"You went behind my back,"
Francesco said harshly.

The bitterness in his voice dulled the edge of her anger. She didn't want to hurt him. She wanted to love him, as she'd done in their first, carefree days.

"You didn't give me any choice," Celia cried. "I had to do it without telling you because you'd have made such a fuss. You always do that if I try to do anything a little bit unusual."

"A little bit?" he echoed. "You were scuba diving. I'm only trying to keep you safe."

"I don't *want* to be safe. I want the freedom to take the same risks as other people, and before I met you I had it. I loved it."

"I don't want to lose you," he growled.

"But you *are* losing me," she said piteously. "Oh, why can't you see that?"

International bestselling author

LUCY GORDON

and
Harlequin Romance®
present

THE
RINUCCI
BROTHERS

Love, marriage…and a family reunited

The Rinucci brothers are back!
Some are related by blood, some not—
but Hope Rinucci thinks of all of them as her sons.

Life has dealt each brother a different hand—some are
happy, some are troubled. But all are handsome, attractive
and successful men, wherever they are in the world.

Meet Carlo, Ruggiero and Francesco
as they find love, marriage—and each other….

Carlo's story,
The Italian's Wife by Sunset:
on sale August 07

Ruggiero's story,
The Mediterranean Rebel's Bride:
on sale October 07

Francesco's story,
The Millionaire Tycoon's English Rose:
on sale December 07

LUCY GORDON
The Millionaire Tycoon's English Rose

THE
RINUCCI
BROTHERS

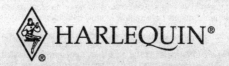

HARLEQUIN®

TORONTO • NEW YORK • LONDON
AMSTERDAM • PARIS • SYDNEY • HAMBURG
STOCKHOLM • ATHENS • TOKYO • MILAN • MADRID
PRAGUE • WARSAW • BUDAPEST • AUCKLAND

ISBN-13: 978-0-373-03992-0
ISBN-10:   0-373-03992-1

THE MILLIONAIRE TYCOON'S ENGLISH ROSE

First North American Publication 2007.

This edition published by arrangement with Harlequin Books S.A.

® and TM are trademarks of the publisher. Trademarks indicated with ® are registered in the United States Patent and Trademark Office, the Canadian Trade Marks Office and in other countries.

www.eHarlequin.com

Printed in U.S.A.

Lucy Gordon cut her writing teeth on magazine journalism, interviewing many of the world's most interesting men, including Warren Beatty, Richard Chamberlain, Roger Moore, Sir Alec Guinness and Sir John Gielgud. She's also camped out with lions in Africa, and has had many other unusual experiences that have often provided the background for her books. She is married to a Venetian, whom she met while on holiday in Venice. They got engaged within two days.

Two of her books have won Romance Writers of America RITA® Awards: *Song of the Lorelei* in 1990, and *His Brother's Child* in 1998, in the Best Traditional Romance category.

You can visit her Web site at www.lucy-gordon.com.

CHAPTER ONE

'*SLIGHTLY to your left…bit more…bit more…reach out now… can you feel it?*'

'Yes,' Celia called in delight.

Her fingers made their way through the water until they touched the rock, eased around it, up, down, exploring in all directions, while the man's voice on the radio spoke in her ear.

'*Try a little farther along. Feel the shape of it.*'

'I've got it,' she said into her own radio. 'Now I want to go down farther.'

Ken, controlling her lightly from on land, asked into the microphone, 'Sure you haven't had enough for the day?'

'I've barely started. I want to do *lots* more yet.'

From the radio in her ear she heard Ken's chuckle as he recognised her familiar cry of 'lots more yet.' It was the mantra by which she lived, her shout of defiance in the face of her blindness. She'd learned it from her blind parents whose motto had been, 'Who needs eyes?'

'I want to go down much deeper,' she said.

He groaned. 'Your boyfriend will murder me.'

'Don't call him my boyfriend as though we were a couple of kids.'

'What, then?'

Good question. What should she call Francesco Rinucci? Her fiancé? No, for they'd never talked about marriage. Her live-in companion? Yes, but that didn't begin to explain it. Her lover? That was true, she thought, shivering pleasurably with the thought. Yes, definitely her lover. But also so much more.

'Don't worry about Francesco,' she said. 'I didn't tell him I was coming here. If he finds out, he'll be too busy murdering me to bother with you. C'mon, let me down. You know I'll be all right.'

'If it's OK with Fiona,' Ken said, naming her diving partner.

'Fine with me,' Fiona sang out on the same frequency. 'Let's go.'

She took Celia's hand and the two of them sank lower and lower into the water of Mount's Bay, just off the coast of Cornwall in England. They, Ken and his crew had set out from Penzance an hour ago, stopping about a mile from the coast in a place that reputedly concealed a sunken pirate galleon.

'Went down in a fierce battle with the British Navy,' he'd told them as they made their way out to sea. 'And they never recovered the treasure, so you may be lucky.'

'You don't need to give me your professional spiel.' Celia had laughed. 'Just having the experience is treasure enough for me.'

She'd forced herself to be patient while they strapped the cylinders onto her back and demonstrated how everything worked. She was wearing a full-face mask, which she had at first resisted.

'I thought it would just be goggles and a mouthpiece connecting me to the oxygen cylinders,' she'd protested.

'Yes, but I want to keep radio contact with you, so you need a full-face mask,' he had said firmly.

She'd yielded under pressure. Then Fiona had taken her hand and the two of them had gone into the water together.

Now Celia could feel her whole body deliciously chilly from the water encasing her outside the rubber suit.

There were more rocks to be felt, plants, sometimes even the exquisite sense of a large fish flapping past, which made her laugh with delight. But the real pleasure lay in the sensation of being free of the world and its tensions.

Free of Francesco Rinucci?

Reluctantly, she admitted that the answer was yes. She adored him, but she'd run away from him as far as she could go. She'd planned this dive a week ago, and kept it a secret from him, saddened by the need, but determined not to yield. If you were blind it was hard enough to keep control of your own life without having to deal with a man who loved you so much that he tried to muffle you in cotton wool.

'All right?' came Fiona's voice over the radio.

'Yes, it's so beautiful,' she said eagerly.

Nobody who knew Celia would be surprised at her saying *beautiful*. She had her own notion of beauty that had nothing to do with eyes. Everything that reached her through the pressure of the water—the coolness and the freedom—all this was beauty.

'You can let me go,' she said, and felt Fiona's hand slip away.

With Ken still holding the other end of the line she wasn't completely free, but she could rely on him to back off as much as possible, and give her the illusion. Francesco could learn so much from him. But Francesco would never face how much he didn't know.

She kicked out with her flippers and powered through the water, relishing the sensation of it streaming past her. Suddenly she was at one with the water, part of it, glorying in it.

'Wheeeeeeee!' she cried.

'Celia?' Ken sounded nervous.

'It's all right,' she said, laughing. 'It's just me going crazy.'

'No change there, then.'

'Nope. Wheeeeeeee!'

'Do you mind?' he complained. 'That was my eardrum.'

She chuckled. 'How far down am I?'

'About a hundred feet.'

'Let me have another forty.'

'Twenty. That's the limit of safety.'

'Twenty-five,' she begged.

'Twenty,' he declared implacably.

The line loosened and she sank farther, reaching out at plants and rocks, anything and everything in this marvellous world.

There had been another time when she'd thought the world was marvellous, when she'd just met Francesco. He'd walked into her workplace and stood talking to the receptionist. Celia had been alerted by a soft, 'Wow!' from Sally, her young assistant, who was sighted.

'Wow?' she queried.

'*Wow!*'

'That's a lot of wow.' Celia chuckled. 'Tell me about him.'

'He's tall and dark with deep blue eyes. Probably late thirties, black hair, waves a bit. I like the way he moves—sort of easy and graceful—and he knows how to wear an expensive suit.'

'You've priced his suit?' Celia'd demanded, amused.

'I've seen it on sale and it costs a fortune. In fact, from the way it fits, I'll bet he had it specially made for him. He's got that sort of something about him. An "air"—like the world is his, he'll take it when it suits him, and in the meantime it can wait until he is ready.'

'You're really studying the subject, aren't you?' Celia'd said, chuckling.

'Naturally I want to give you an accurate description. Oh, yes, and he's got a brooding look that you only see in film stars— Oh, gosh, I forgot you haven't seen any film stars. I'm really sorry.'

'Don't apologise,' Celia'd said warmly. 'I work hard to make people forget that I can't see. You just told me I've succeeded. But I've always been blind, so I can't imagine anything. I don't know what colours look like, or shapes and sizes. I have to discover them by touch.'

'Well, his shape and size would really be worth discovering by touch,' Sally'd said frankly, and Celia'd burst into a peal of laughter.

'He's looking this way,' Sally'd hissed. 'Now he's coming over.'

Next thing Celia heard a quiet, deep voice with the hint of an Italian accent. 'Good morning. My name is Francesco Rinucci. I'm looking for Celia Ryland.'

The moment she heard his voice she could 'see' him—not in the kind of detail Sally had explained, but in her own way. Easy and graceful, an air as though the world was his; those she had understood at once.

Now, making her way through the water and remembering, she thought that the world really had been his. And when she was in his arms, the world had been hers.

But that had been five months ago. In five short months she'd loved him passionately, fought with him furiously, and learned that she must escape him at all costs.

Five months, and so much had happened in between. So much joy, so much bitterness, so much regret that they had ever met, so much thankfulness that she had known him even for a brief time.

She remembered everything of their meeting. Details

reached her differently from other people, but more intensely. As was her way, she had been the first to offer her hand, and had felt him clasp it in return. His hand felt strong and good, with long fingers and a feeling of suppressed power. It had made her wonder about the rest of him.

'Worth discovering by touch,' Sally had said.

Celia had tried to put the thought out of her mind but without success. She'd been vividly aware of him moving carefully in the confined space near her desk, where much of the room had been taken up by Wicksy, her golden Labrador guide dog.

Wicksy's manners were beautiful but reticent. He had accepted Francesco's admiration as his due, returned it to the extent of briefly resting his snout in Francesco's hand, then returned to curling up beneath Celia's desk, apparently relaxed but actually on guard.

The newcomer had sat down close to her, and she'd been able to sense his height, the breadth of him, and something else, a pleasing aroma that shifted between spice and wood-smoke, borne by the breeze. It had spoken of warmth and life, and it had told her that she was living in a shell and should try to reach outside, where he might be waiting.

Only might?

It would be a chance worth taking.

'Why were you looking for me?' she asked.

He explained that he was part of Tallis Inc., a firm famous for the manufacture of luxury furniture. Its wares were excellent and it was expanding all over Europe.

'We need a good PR firm,' he said. 'The one we're using has gone downhill. I was advised to come here, and to ask for you personally. They say you're the best.'

Being a gentleman, he made a valiant effort to keep the surprise out of his voice, without quite managing it.

'And now you're wondering why someone didn't warn you that I was blind?' she said impishly.

That threw him; she could tell. She burst out laughing.

'No—I wasn't—' he said hastily.

'Oh, yes, you were. Don't deny it to me. I've been here too often. I know what people think when they meet me unawares.'

'Am I that easy to read?' His tone suggested a hesitant smile.

'Right this minute you're thinking, How the hell did I get into this, and how am I going to get out without being rude?'

It was a favourite joke of hers—to read their minds, trip them up, make them feel a little uneasy.

But he wasn't uneasy. He took her hand and held it tightly, speaking seriously.

'No, I'm not thinking that. I don't think you could guess what I'm thinking.'

He was wrong. She could guess exactly. Because she was thinking the same thing.

It was unnerving to find such thoughts possessing her about a man she'd only just met, but she couldn't help herself. And a part of her, the part that rushed to meet adventure, wasn't sorry at all. True, another part of her counselled caution, but she was used to ignoring it.

But for the moment she must act with propriety, so she showed him the array of equipment that helped her to function.

'I talk to the computer and it talks back to me,' Celia said. 'Plus I have a special phone, and various other things.'

He took her to lunch at a small restaurant next door, and he talked about his firm while she tapped information into a small terminal. Afterwards he began to walk her back to the office, but she stopped, saying, 'I have to take Wicksy to the park.'

He went with her, watching, fascinated, as she plunged into her bag and brought out a ball.

'If I throw it now, I won't hit anyone, will I?' she asked anxiously.

He assured her she wouldn't, then wished he'd been more cautious. Instead of the ladylike gesture he'd expected, she put all her force into hurling the ball a great distance, so that a man contentedly munching sandwiches had to jump out of the way with an angry yell.

'You told me it was safe,' she said in mock complaint.

'I'm sorry. I didn't realise you could throw that far.'

With a bark of joy, Wicksy bounded after the ball, retrieved it and charged back to drop it at her feet. After another couple of throws he came to sit before her, his head cocked to one side, gazing up at her with a significant expression.

'All right, let's go,' she said, taking the ball from his mouth and putting it away. 'This next bit is rather indelicate, so you may want to go away.'

'I'll be brave,' he said, grinning.

She found a spot under the trees, said, 'OK, go on,' and Wicksy obeyed while she reached into her bag for the scoop and plastic bag.

'Would you like me to do that for you?' he asked through gritted teeth.

'That's being gallant above and beyond the call of duty,' she said, liking him for it. 'But he's my responsibility and I'll wield the pooper-scooper.'

'Well, I offered,' he said, and something in the sound of the words told her he was grinning with relief.

When the business was complete they made their way back across the park.

At the door of her building he said, 'I meant to tell you a lot more about my firm and our requirements, but there wasn't time. Can I take you to dinner tonight and we can talk some more?'

'I would like that.'

She spent the rest of the afternoon hard at work, for she wanted to impress him. Then she went home, showered, and put on a gold dress that she'd been told looked stunning with her red hair.

In the apartment next door lived Angela, a good friend who worked in a wholesale fashion house, and one of the few people Celia trusted enough to ask for help. Having called her in, she twisted and turned before her.

'Will I do?'

'Oh, yes, you'll do, and then some. You look gorgeous. I was right to make you get that dress. And those sandals. Lord, but I envy you your long legs and your ankles. If you knew how rare it is for a woman to have ankles as slender as yours, and yet have perfect balance so that you can walk on them without wobbling! I could murder you for that alone.'

Celia chuckled. She owed Angela a lot, for it was she who'd taught her how to win the admiring glances that she knew followed her even without seeing them. Angela had decreed the colours that went with Celia's red hair.

'But what does it mean—red hair?' Celia had asked.

'It means you've got to be very careful what you wear with it. You're lucky in your complexion, pale and delicate, the perfect English-rose style.'

'What's an English rose?' Celia had asked at once.

'Let's just say men go for it. That's what you're hoping for, isn't it?'

'Certainly not. This is a business meeting to discuss strategy and forward planning.'

'Boy, you really have got it bad.'

Celia laughed, but inwardly she could feel herself blushing. Her friend's words were true. She had got it bad already.

When she opened the door to Francesco that evening she heard what she'd been hoping for—a brief hesitation that said he was taken aback by her appearance. She smiled at his wolf whistle and inclined her head in mock acceptance.

There was the tiniest hint of their future disagreements when he wanted her to leave Wicksy behind.

'He goes with me everywhere,' she said firmly

'Surely he doesn't have to? I'll keep you safe.'

'But I don't want to be kept safe,' she said, still smiling. 'Wicksy treats me as an equal in ways that nobody else does.'

'But you don't need him if you've got me,' he insisted. 'Besides, restaurants don't like dogs.'

'There's one two streets away that knows Wicksy and always welcomes him. Let's not argue about it. Wicksy belongs with me and I belong with him.'

She kept her tone pleasant, but he must have sensed her determination because he yielded. She knew a twinge of disappointment. Understanding her need for independence was one of her silent 'tests' and he'd failed it. But there was time yet, and she was determined to enjoy her evening with him.

They walked the short distance to the restaurant, and settled down at their table to talk.

'Did you have to bring that great folder in with you?' he asked.

'Of course. How else could I make my pitch? This is a working dinner, remember? I have several ideas that I think you'll like.'

She talked for several minutes, illustrating her points by pushing various pages towards him. She'd earlier marked them with nail scissors, so that she could tell by feel which was which.

'You seem to know everything about everything we've ever made,' he said, awed.

'I've been working hard.'

'I can tell, but how on earth—' he asked.

'I accessed a lot of information about your firm on line this afternoon.'

'And your computer delivers it vocally?' he hazarded.

'There is software that does that,' she said vaguely.

In truth she'd got Sally to read it out to her, a method she sometimes used when she was short of time. But she wasn't going to tell him that.

There were two conversations going on here, she realised. On the surface she sold her abilities, while he admired her work. It was pleasant, restrained, but beneath the surface they were sizing each other up.

Celia listened closely to every nuance of his voice. Without being deep, it had a resonance that excited her and made her want to touch him.

She'd chosen this restaurant and insisted on taking Wicksy because in that way she could keep some sort of control. The trouble was that she increasingly wanted to abandon control and hurl herself headlong into the unknown.

She sensed that he, too, was putting a brake on himself, but his caution was greater than hers. Francesco eased her away from the subject of work, and made her talk about herself.

'How did your parents cope with you being blind?' he asked.

'Easily. They were both blind, too,' she explained.

'*Mio Dio!* How terrible!' he said instinctively.

'Not really. You'd be amazed how little you miss what you've never had. Since they couldn't see, either, and I'm an only child, I had almost no point of comparison. The three of us formed a kind of secret society. It was us against the world because we thought everyone else was crazy. They thought we were crazy, too, because we wouldn't conform to their ideas about how blind people ought to behave.

'They met at university, where he was a young professor and she was one of his students. He writes books now, and she does his secretarial work. He says she's more efficient than any sighted secretary because she knows what to watch out for. They used to say they fell in love because they understood things that nobody else did. So I grew up accepting the way we lived as normal, and I still do.'

There was a slight warning in her voice as she said the last words, but she didn't make much of the point.

She managed to turn the conversation towards him. He told her about his family in Italy, his parents and his five brothers, the villa perched on the hill with the view over the Bay of Naples. Then he caught himself up, embarrassed.

'It's all right,' she told him. 'I don't expect people to censor their speech because I've never seen the things they describe. If I did that I wouldn't have any friends.'

'And you've never seen anything of the world at all,' he said in wonder. 'That's what I can't get my head round.'

'Yes, I suppose it is hard,' she mused. 'This morning my friend told me you had deep blue eyes, but I had to tell her I couldn't picture them.'

In the brief silence she could sense him looking around, and strove not to smile.

'Why—did she tell you that?' he asked, almost nervously.

She assumed a wicked, breathy innocence. 'You mean, it's not true? Your eyes are really deep red?'

'Only when I've had too much to drink.'

She laughed so much that Wicksy, dozing at her feet, pushed his snout against her, asking if all was well.

Something other than laughter was happening that evening.

It was in the air between them. Another woman might have read it in his eyes. Celia sensed it with the whole of her being.

The talk drifted back to his family.

'My mother's English, but you'd never know it. At heart Signora Rinucci is a real Italian *mamma,* determined to marry all her sons off.'

'Six sons? That's quite an undertaking. How's she doing?'

'Four married, two left, But my brother Ruggiero has just got engaged. He'll marry Polly fairly soon, and then Mamma will turn her firepower on me.'

So now he'd contrived to let her know that he wasn't married, she thought, appreciating his tactics.

'Don't your parents do the same with you?' he asked casually.

'It's the one thing they've never given me advice about,' she said. 'Except when Dad's been at work in the kitchen Mum will say, "Never marry a man who cooks squid." And she's right.'

After a brief silence he said, 'We have squid in the Bay of Naples. Best in the world, so the fishermen say.'

'But you don't cook it, do you?'

'No, I don't cook it,' he assured her.

And then a strange silence fell, slightly touched by embarrassment, as though they'd both strayed closer to danger than they'd meant.

Celia found that she couldn't be the one to break the silence, because she was so conscious of what had caused it, but his manner of breaking it brought no comfort. He offered her coffee and another glass of wine, his manner polite and impeccable. Earlier he'd been warm and pleasant. Suddenly only courtesy was left, and it had a hollow feel.

The truth began to creep over her, and with it a chill.

At her front door he said, 'I'll take your folder with me. I like your ideas, and I think we've got a deal, but I'll know more when I've read it again.'

'You've got my number?'

'I made sure I got it. Good night.'

He didn't even try to kiss her.

Now she knew the truth.

When he didn't call her, she understood why. As though she was inside his head, she followed his thoughts, his dread of getting too close to a blind woman, his common sense advice to himself to back off now, before it was too late.

'They all do it,' she mused to Wicksy as they took their final walk one evening. She sat on a bench beneath the trees and felt him press against her. 'We've both known it to happen before. Remember Joe? You never liked him, did you? You tried to tell me that he wouldn't last, and you were right.'

His nose was cold and comforting in her hand.

'Men are scared to become involved with me in case it disrupts their pleasant lives, their successful careers.'

The nose nudged gently.

'I know,' she said sadly. 'We can't blame them, can we? And maybe it's better for him to be honest and retreat now rather than later.'

Another soft nudge.

'It's just that I thought this time it might have been different. I thought *he* was different. But he isn't.'

There was a whine from beside her knee, with a distant air of urgency.

'What's that? Oh, the biscuit. I'm sorry. I forgot. Here.'

She felt it vanish from her hand.

'What would I do without you, my darling? You've got more sense than the rest of us put together. As long as I've got you, I don't need anyone else.'

Celia leaned down and rested her cheek against his head, trying to take comfort from their loving companionship.

But the truth was that her heart was aching. Something about Francesco had reached out to her, and she had reached back because it had felt so right. It was crazy to feel like this about a man she'd only just met, but with all her heart and soul she wanted him.

Now, floating in the blessed anonymity of the ocean, she wondered how she could have loved him so agonisingly then, and five months later be running away from him?

The question tortured her as she sank deeper into the water, reliving the events of yesterday, when she'd slipped out of the home they shared without telling him where she was going. She'd left him a note that she'd managed to write on a large pad:

I'LL CALL YOU LATER TODAY, CELIA.

She'd hated the deception, hated herself for doing it, but she'd had no choice. She loved him now as much as she'd done on that evening, five months ago, when she'd wondered, sadly, if she would ever see him again. If anything, she loved him more.

And yet she'd escaped him, knowing that if she didn't she would go mad.

CHAPTER TWO

THE PR contract had been arranged the next day, and over the following week there had been a good deal of coming and going between the two firms. But it had never been Francesco who arrived. Celia had resigned herself to not meeting him again when there was a knock on her front door in the evening.

She'd gone to the door, switching on the light as she went, so that the visitor should have some illumination. She lived without lights.

'Who is it?' she called.

'It's me,' came his voice from behind the door.

He didn't need to identify himself further. They both understood that there was only one 'me.' She opened the door and put out her hand, feeling it enfolded in his.

'I came because—' He stopped. 'There are things we need to— Will you let me in—*please?*'

She stood back. 'Come in.'

She heard the click as the door closed behind him. He was still holding her hand, but for a moment he didn't move, as if he was unsure what would come next.

'I didn't think you'd come back,' she said. 'The contract—'

'The hell with the contract,' he said with soft violence. 'Do you really think that's why I'm here?'

'I don't know what to think,' she whispered. 'I haven't known all week.'

'I'll tell you what to think of me—that I'm a coward who runs away from a woman who's different, more challenging than other women. I run away because secretly I'm afraid I can't match up to her. I just know I'll let her down and she'll be better off without me—'

'Isn't that for her to decide?' she asked joyfully.

His hand tightened on hers and she felt him raise it, then his lips against her palm.

'I couldn't keep away from you,' he said huskily. 'I tried, but I can't. And I never will be able to.'

'I'll never want you to,' she said in passionate gratitude.

His lips were burning her hand, igniting her whole body so that she longed for him to touch her everywhere. She drew his face towards her and felt the urgency of his mouth at the first touch of hers. It was as though she'd given him the signal he'd been waiting for.

Now she knew that she'd wanted this since she'd sat with him in the restaurant, listening to his words and trying to picture the mouth that shaped them. His lips on hers, coaxing, inciting, urging, pleading, had been the temptation that teased and taunted her.

And all this week, after he'd gone, she'd been haunted by dreams of the impossible, of his body lying naked against her in the equality that darkness would bring. Now he was here, and joy and excitement possessed her body and soul.

'Celia,' he said huskily. 'Celia—'

She stepped back, drawing him after her towards the bedroom, reaching up to turn out the hall light, so that the place was dark again and only she knew the way.

It might be madness to rush helter-skelter into love.

Caution was indicated. But her circumstances and a combative nature had always made her despise caution. Besides, Francesco had tried it and it didn't work. It was a relief, setting her free.

She touched his face, letting her fingers gently explore its planes and angles, the wide mouth and sharply defined jaw, the slightly crooked nose. He was just as she wanted him to be.

She remembered everything. Floating now on the cushion of water, cut off from the world, she recalled details that she'd barely noticed at the time. They'd been obscured by the sweet fire flaming through her, engulfing all in its path, yet they'd endured in some corner of her consciousness, to be relived later.

Now they made her heart ache for their cruel contrast with the present. Francesco was still the same man who'd won her love by his gentleness and his open adoration of her. He was still the man who'd taken her to bed and loved her with slow, reverent gestures that had brought her flesh to eager life.

The pressure of the water on every part of her body was bringing back those memories. With his very first touch she had felt that he was touching her everywhere. As his lips had lain gently against her breast the reaction had flowed up from her loins and out to every part.

She had been eager to welcome him in, reaching for him, drawing him close, moving with his rhythm. Everything had felt natural because it was with him. His skin, touching hers, had been warm, growing more heated as his passion mounted.

To make love in blindness was an act of trust, but hadn't failed her. He had been a tender lover, gentle, considerate even in the intensity of his ardour, and above all, generous. Looking back, she often said that her passion had started the day they'd met. Her love dated from that first night together.

When the first explosion of delight had been over and they

had fallen apart, stunned and joyful, she'd propped herself up on one elbow and begun to explore him.

'After all, I can't see you,' she teased. 'I have to find out in my own way.'

'I guess you were going to discover my feeble muscles and pot-belly some time or other.' He laughed.

'Yup. Let's see, now, is this your shoulder?'

'It's at the top of my arm, so I guess it must be.'

'Nothing feeble about that muscle,' she murmured. 'And it continues very nicely along here.'

'You've left my arm behind. That's my chest.'

'Mmm,' she whispered, kissing the pectoral muscles one by one. 'You don't have any hair on your chest. I prefer that.'

'Are you saying you're an expert?'

'Blind teaching is very modern these days,' she said in a serious voice. 'We take lessons in everything.'

There was the briefest pause before he said cautiously, 'Everything?'

'Almost everything.'

'Are you making fun of me?'

Her lips twitched. 'Do you think I am?'

'I wish I could be sure.'

'Well, you can decide about that later. Where was I?'

'Exploring my chest.'

'Let's leave that for the moment. I don't want to rush this.'

'I don't want to rush it, either,' he said huskily, letting her fingers roam over his thighs, relishing every moment.

'You have very long legs,' she murmured in a considering voice. 'At least, I suppose they are. I don't have many points of comparison.'

'I wish you didn't have any—unless, of course, you learned that in the leg class?'

She stifled her laughter against his chest, and at last she felt him relax enough to laugh, as well.

Francesco didn't relax easily, she could tell. It had been a real shock to him when she'd made a joke about her blindness, but he'd soon get the hang of that. She would teach him. In the meantime, they had other business.

'Now, about that pot-belly of yours,' she murmured, letting her fingers continue their work. 'It doesn't feel very pot to me.'

'I don't keep it precisely there,' he said in a tense voice.

'You want me to move?'

'No, just…keep doing…what you're doing.'

She did as he wished, realising that their previous loving had barely taken the edge off his passion and he was once more in a state of heated arousal. He was hard and hot in her palm, and she indulged herself in pleasure until, at the precise moment she intended, he lost control and tossed her onto her back.

Her own control was fast vanishing. She was eager for him to move over her and repeat the experience that had been so thrilling the first time. She reached for him, barely able to contain herself, clasping him so firmly that they were united in an instant.

At the feel of him inside her she gave a shout of pleasure that mingled with his and began to move strongly, urgently, wrapping her legs around him and holding him close. She wanted to keep him like that always.

Afterwards they slept in each other's arms for a couple of hours and awoke hungry. She went into the kitchen, refusing his offer to make the food himself.

'I know where everything is,' she assured him.

'Yes, you just proved that,' he murmured.

'Don't be vulgar.' She chuckled, aiming a mock punch at him.

But she misjudged the distance and caught him across the face, making him yell more in surprise than pain.

'Darling, darling, I'm sorry,' she cried, kissing him fiercely. 'I didn't mean that.'

'You're a violent woman,' he complained.

'No, just a blind one. You'll be covered in bruises in no time.'

'How can you talk like that?'

'Because it's true. You should escape me now, while you still can!'

'I didn't mean that. I meant the other thing.'

'About being blind?'

'Yes. Never mind that now. Let's have something to eat.'

She made sandwiches and coffee and they picnicked in the bedroom.

'It upsets you when I make jokes about being blind, doesn't it?' she mused, munching.

'It confuses me. It's like invading sacred ground.'

'It's not sacred to me. Anyway, it's my ground and I'll invade it if I want to. And if I can, you can. So hush!'

They had laughed, and loved again, laughed again and loved again. That was how it had been in the beginning.

And even then the first danger signs had been there, but they'd both been too much in love to heed them. If only...

'*Time to come in,*' came the voice over the radio.

'Just a few more minutes,' Celia begged.

'*Your air will be running out soon. Did you find any pirate treasure?*'

'Not this time, but I always live in hope,' she said, determinedly cheerful.

It was time to go back and face the world. Fiona was close by, calling her, and together they made their way to the boat, where hands came down to welcome them aboard.

'How was it?' Ken asked.

'Wonderful!' Celia exclaimed. 'The most glorious

feeling—being weightless, and so free—such freedom—as though the rest of the world didn't exist.'

'Is that your idea of freedom?' Fiona asked. 'Escaping the rest of the world?'

'Escaping the world's prejudices, yes,' Celia murmured thoughtfully.

'Ah,' Ken said in a significant voice. 'I'm afraid that the world has followed you here. I've just heard on the radio that when we get back to land you'll find Francesco waiting for you.'

'How did he find me here? I just said I was going. I didn't say where.'

'I guess he's got a very good surveillance team working on it,' Ken suggested lightly.

He meant it as a joke, but Celia's face tightened and her voice was hard as she said, 'Evidently.'

'What do you want to do?' Ken asked. 'You've paid for the whole day, and there's two hours left, so we don't have to go back before then.'

It was on the tip of her tongue to tell him to head out to sea for a long as possible. But she mastered the impulse and said in a resigned voice, 'No, let's go back now. I've got to face him sooner or later.'

'Why have you got to face him?' Fiona asked indignantly. 'This is the twenty-first century. A woman doesn't have to put up with an abusive man.'

'But he isn't abusive.' Celia sighed. 'He's gentle and loving and protective. He wants to shield me from every wind that blows.'

'Oh, Lord!' Fiona said in sympathy. As they neared land she said, 'I can see his face now. He doesn't look loving and protective. He looks mad as hell.'

'Good!' Celia said. 'Then can I be as mad as hell and throw something at him?'

'What would you do about aiming?' Fiona wanted to know.

'I wouldn't need to,' Celia said despairingly. 'If he saw me lifting a heavy vase he'd get in front of me and let it hit him. *Ooooh, what am I going to do with a man like that?*'

'Leave him,' Fiona said at once. 'Or you won't survive.'

'I know, I *know,* but it's so drastic.'

'Yes, but I know what it's like. I broke my leg once, and my boyfriend drove me crazy fussing round me—do this, don't do that, let me get this for you, don't strain yourself. In the end I thumped him with my crutch. It was the only way.'

'What happened to him?' Celia asked, fascinated.

'Don't know. I never saw him again.'

Celia laughed, but the laughter soon faded and she leaned on the rail, her head bent down in the direction of the water that she could hear foaming beneath.

When they reached their destination Francesco was the first on board, coming straight to her and taking her hand.

'I'll take you ashore,' he said. 'And we'll go home.'

'No, thank you,' she replied firmly. 'As part of my day out I get a meal with the crew. And I'm hungry.'

'I'll get you a meal on the way home,' he persisted.

His hands were on her arms, urging her so firmly that her anger began to grow.

'Let go of me, Francesco,' she said in a low voice.

'I only want to guide you—'

'So you say. But you're that close to dragging me. Please let go, because I'm going to eat here.'

'If it makes it any easier we'll give you a refund for that part of the fee,' Ken offered.

It actually made things harder for her, by cutting the ground out from under her feet, making her sound childishly stubborn for the sake of it. But he meant well, so she smiled and yielded.

She was forced to let Francesco help her off the boat and escort her towards the changing rooms. But she knew he was waiting for her outside. She must face him. And then what?

She knew him so well. She could feel his moods tearing apart the darkness around her, and could sense that behind his courteous charm he was in a furious temper that he was determined to conceal. She, too, was in a temper, but less sure about the virtue of concealing it.

Celia said her goodbyes and thanked Ken for a wonderful day.

'And I don't want a refund,' she said. 'I had a great time.'

'Er—actually, I've already given the refund to your friend.'

'*What?* I never said I was going to agree.'

'He thought he was doing what would please you,' Ken said placatingly.

'You mean, he took it for granted that he knew best,' Celia snapped. 'How much did you give him?'

He told her, and she immediately plunged into her bag and produced the amount.

'I do not want a refund,' she said.

'Celia, c'mon—'

'*Take it!*'

One look at her set face was enough to make him accept the notes.

'Good,' she said. 'Now, where's the driver I hired for the day? He should be here to take me home.'

'I'm here,' said the voice of a middle-aged man beside her. 'But there's a feller over there keeps trying to make me go away. He says he'll drive you. But I can't just go off unless you say so. What should I do?'

For a moment she was on the verge of getting into the car

and leaving Francesco standing there, looking foolish. But the impulse died. This wasn't the time nor the place for the coming battle.

'Tell him you'll do what he wants,' she said. 'But only in return for a huge tip.'

'How huge?'

'Take him for all you can,' she said crossly.

'Yes, *ma'am!*'

'Remind me never to get on your wrong side,' Ken said with feeling.

She laughed reluctantly. 'Yes, I'm told I scare strong men.'

'I believe it. But here's Fiona with Wicksy. He isn't scared of you.'

Her guide dog came forward, relieved at recovering her after an absence of several hours. For a few moments they nuzzled each other.

'Sorry to leave you alone, my darling,' she murmured. 'I couldn't take you onto the boat—'

'I think he'd have jumped into the water after you,' Ken said.

'Yes, he would,' he said fondly.

'Are you ready?' That was Francesco's voice. 'I'm driving you home.'

'What about the driver I hired?' Celia asked, contriving to sound innocent.

'I persuaded him to go.'

'You had no right to do that.'

'Then no doubt you'll be pleased to know that he exacted a hefty price,' Francesco said grimly.

'Really? Shocking!'

'And don't try to sound surprised, because I saw him talking to you, and it wouldn't surprise me to learn that you put him up to that bit of blackmail.'

'Who? Me?'

'Here's the car. In you go, boy.'

When Wicksy was safely installed on the backseat Celia got into the front, immediately feeling his cold nose against her neck—his way of reminding her that he was still here. She put her hand behind her to touch him, silently saying, Message received, and after that they were both able to relax.

She needed all Wicksy's calming influence to silence her inner rage at what Francesco had done. It was a long drive home, and she didn't want to fight in the car.

At first it seemed he didn't want to, either, but after a while he said through gritted teeth, 'How could you? How could you do it?'

'I did it because I had to. Because I wanted to find out if I *could.*'

'And now you know. Is anything better?'

'It might have been if you hadn't spoiled it. I could just as easily ask, How could *you?* No, no, don't answer that. We mustn't fight about this now. We've said it all so often. Let's just get home.'

Nobody spoke for the rest of the drive, but it didn't feel like silence because the air was jagged with anger and with all the words being suppressed. By the time they reached their destination she was exhausted.

Home was still the flat she'd lived in before, which had been adapted for her in so many ways that it had made sense for him to move in with her five months earlier. After that one sweet loving there had been no question about their living together. Neither of them could have borne to do anything else.

'I'll take Wicksy for his walk,' she said as she got out of the car.

'I'll come with you.'

'*No!*' The word came out in a flash, before she could stop it, and she was instantly contrite. 'I'm sorry—it's just that I need to be alone. I'm all tensed up.'

'I'll be waiting at home, then,' he said in a colourless voice.

She was out for a long time, deliberately delaying her return home because of the fearful voice in her mind that warned her they were approaching a crisis, and the wrong words could destroy them both.

Part of her knew the problem had to be faced, and she wanted to go forward and deal with it. Part of her shrank away, arguing that things could be smoothed over with more time, and perhaps everything would be better in future. He might even be asleep when she returned.

But he wasn't asleep, and she knew that the evil moment couldn't be postponed any longer.

'You were gone a long time,' he said edgily. 'I was—'

'Don't!' she told him quickly. 'Don't say you were worried about me. Just don't say that.'

'Is it wrong for me to be worried about you?'

'You overdo it. That's all I meant.'

'I know what a tough day you've had, and when you vanish into the darkness like that—'

'Francesco, for pity's sake,' she groaned. 'Why do you say things like that?'

'Like what?'

'Vanish into the darkness. I'm always in the darkness. It's where I'm at home. I'm not lost in it, as you would be. Why can't I make you understand that?'

'I do understand it in one way—'

'It's not enough,' she cried. 'I'm not helpless, I'm not an invalid, but in your mind I'm always slightly less than a whole person.'

'No—not really. But—you do have a disadvantage that other people don't have—'

'I also have advantages that other people don't have. My memory is twice as good as yours, because I've trained it. I can hear things in people's voices that you'd miss. I saved you a lot of money once by warning you that the man you were planning to do business with was untrustworthy. I could hear it in his voice. You were very lofty about that at the time. "You and your intuition!" you said. But at least you had the sense to listen to me and throw him out. He's just started a two-year stretch for fraud, in case you didn't know.'

'Yes, I did. I was going to tell you, and say thank you. But I might have known you'd hear it first.'

'Yes, you might. Perhaps I'm not as much at a disadvantage as you think.'

He sighed, and she could hear him pacing the room.

'How did you know where to find me?' she asked.

'I remembered Ken from when we met him at that party. You talked to him for so long that I got jealous—until I realised it was his diving that fascinated you. You've called him several times since then, haven't you?'

'Yes, I have. It took time to set up today.'

'I'm sure there must have been a lot of planning,' he said in a bleak voice. 'Booking the day, hiring the car to drive you down there, leaving the flat secretly, not telling me where you were going—that took some organising. When I found your note I checked up on Ken's firm and discovered that you had a booking.'

'So you jumped into your car and came down to tell me that I mustn't dive because I didn't have your permission?' she said through gritted teeth.

'Because it isn't safe for you.'

'It's as safe for me as for anyone. I was on a line. Ken could have hauled me in at any time.'

'You went behind my back,' he said harshly.

The bitterness in his voice dulled the edge of her anger, reminding her how easy it was to hurt him. She didn't want to hurt him, She wanted to love him as she'd done in their first carefree days; days that she knew would never come again.

'You don't give me any choice,' she cried. 'I had to do it without telling you because you'd have made such a fuss. You always do that if I try to do anything a little bit unusual.'

'A little bit?' he echoed. 'You were scuba diving.'

'Yes, and I managed perfectly well. As I knew I would. But you can't bring yourself to believe that, can you? Sometimes I think you actually hate it when I manage to do something without you.'

'For God's sake, do you know what you're saying?'

'Yes, I'm saying I want to live my life as an adult, without having to apply to you for permission to take every breath.'

'I'm only trying to keep you safe.'

'I don't *want* to be safe. I want the freedom to take the same risks as other people, and before I met you I had it. I loved it. But you set yourself to take it away from me, wrap me in cotton wool and lock me in a cocoon. I can't live in there, Francesco, not even if you're there with me. It's like a prison, and I have to break out.'

'Aren't you being a bit melodramatic?' he demanded

'Not from where I'm standing.'

'Meaning that I'm a gaoler?'

'The kindest, most loving gaoler in the world,' she said, trying to soften it. 'I know that you love me, and it's your love that makes you overprotective, but I can't live that way. I've got to get as far out on the edge as I can without you trying to drag me back.'

'Drag you— Now you're talking nonsense.'

'Anything you disagree with is nonsense, according to you. I can't live my life wondering if you're standing there behind me, trying to bring everything to a halt.'

'You don't—'

'Francesco, listen to me, please. The really sad thing about today is that I would have loved to share it with you. It would have been wonderful to go into the water together and sink down, hand in hand. I even came to the edge of telling you. But I backed off at the last minute because I knew you'd do everything to stop me.'

'Because I don't want to lose you,' he growled.

'But you *are* losing me,' she said piteously. 'Oh, why can't you see that?'

'By trying to protect you? Isn't that my job? We're practically husband and wife, and a man looks after his wife—'

'That shouldn't mean putting a ball and chain on her.'

She heard his sharp intake of breath. 'That's a lousy thing to say.'

'I'm sorry. I didn't mean it like that.'

'I'd sure as hell like to know how you did mean it,' he said bitterly.

'It's just that to you life is one big word—*no*.'

'All right, maybe I take things a little too far,' he grated, 'but I don't just ask *you* to say no to things you want. I wouldn't do that without being prepared to do the same.'

'What do you mean by that?' she asked, with a sudden keen edge to her voice.

He failed to hear its significance,

'My firm asked me to start an Italian branch, in Naples—'

'Your home town,' she gasped in delight. 'That's great. When do we leave?'

'We don't. I turned it down.'

'You did what?'

'How could I possibly ask you to come to Italy with me? You manage well enough in England, but what would you do in a strange country?'

'Meaning that I'm too stupid to find the way? Are you forgetting that I've already learned Italian?'

'We've done some together, *cara,* and it's been delight-ful—'

'A delightful game, you mean?' she said in a hard voice. 'Humouring me. You made a big decision like that without consulting me because you didn't think I was up to the task?'

'I only meant—'

'How dare you? *How dare you?*'

'I was only thinking of you,' he retorted.

'Did I ask you to think of me? I'm not a child, Francesco, and I'm not an idiot. And I've had enough of you treating me that way.'

'Look, we'll talk about it when you've calmed down.'

'I'm not worked up. Inside I'm as cold as ice, and I'm telling you that I want you to go.'

'Go where? I live here.'

'Not any longer. It doesn't work between us. I think perhaps it never could. Please go quickly. I don't want to see you here again.'

'You don't want to *what?*'

'Go!'

'Celia, for pity's sake, stop this before it's too late.'

'It's been too late for a long time,' she whispered.

'Look, I'm sorry if I went too far. But after all we've been to each other you can't just—'

'It's over,' she said, feeling that she would start to scream in a minute. 'Please go, Francesco. Just pack a bag and go tonight. You can get the rest of your things later. But go now.'

In the silence she could sense that he was totally stunned. He knew she meant it.

Suddenly she broke.

'*Get out!*' she screamed. '*Just get out!*'

CHAPTER THREE

'GET out. Just get out.'

He heard the words before he awoke. They echoed in the darkness behind his eyes, screaming around his head like curses.

Then his eyes were open and he was sitting up in bed, trying to understand the world around him. He didn't know where he was. Surely this was his home back in London, but where was she? Why not in bed with him?

Then the haze cleared, the walls fell into place. He was back at his parents' home, the Villa Rinucci in southern Italy, a place where he hadn't lived for years.

Now he was using it as a refuge until he could clear his head. Nothing had been straight in his mind since the day Celia had thrown him out. Somehow he'd organised himself, agreed to return to Naples to set up the Italian branch of his firm, and left England. There had been one brief meeting with Celia when he'd collected his things, but they had spoken to each other like strangers, and he hadn't seen her again. She was behind him. Finished. Over and done with.

Except that her cry of *'Get out!'* still echoed with him, day and night. And the worst thing, the thing that actually scared him, was that it wasn't only her voice he heard. It was as though someone had cast a malign spell, triggered by those words and those alone. And he couldn't escape.

Francesco got out of bed and went to the window, seeing the dawn beginning to break over the Bay of Naples. As he sat there, unwilling to return to bed and risk a repetition of the nightmare, he heard a soft footstep in the corridor outside and knew that it was Hope, refusing to accept that a man in his late-thirties didn't need to be hovered over protectively by his mother.

He heard her stop outside his door and waited with dread for the knock. He loved his mother, but he shrank from the questions he couldn't answer because he didn't want to face them.

After a while she went away, leaving him alone with the brightening dawn that had no power over the darkness inside him.

'Are you looking at those again?' Toni Rinucci asked his wife warmly.

Hope smiled, looking up from the book of wedding photographs she was studying.

'I can't help it,' she said. 'They are so beautiful.'

'But Ruggiero has been married for three months now,' he said, naming one of their twin sons.

'The pictures are still beautiful after three months,' Hope said. 'Look at little Matti.'

Ruggiero's toddler son stood just in front of his father and Polly, his new stepmother. Although only two years old, he'd already managed to steal the limelight.

'He looks like a little angel in that pageboy suit,' Hope said sentimentally.

'Yes—you'd never know that he'd covered it with mud ten minutes later,' Toni observed with grandfatherly cynicism.

'He's real boy,' Hope declared happily. 'Oh, look!'

She'd reached the picture showing all six of her sons.

'It's so good to see them all together.' She sighed. 'Francesco has been away so much—first America, then England—but this time he was here. Oh, it's so good to have him finally back where he belongs.'

Toni was silent as they went down the stairs together, and Hope, who could read his silences, glanced at him.

'You don't think so?' she asked.

'I'm not sure he's home to stay. He's not a boy any more.'

'But of course he won't stay with us for ever,' Hope conceded. 'He'll find his own place and move out. But we'll still see him far more often than when he was living abroad.'

Hope made some coffee for the two of them, and took it out onto the terrace with its view over the bay. They both loved these moments when they had the house to themselves and could indulge in gossip about everyday matters—their household, their sons, their growing army of grandchildren, their upcoming thirty-fifth wedding anniversary—or just about nothing in particular.

'That isn't really what I meant,' said Toni as she set his coffee before him, just as he liked it. 'I sense something strange about his coming home now.'

'He came home for the wedding,' Hope pointed out.

'Yes, but we thought he'd be here a few days, and bring Celia with him. Instead, he came without her, and stayed. Why did he suddenly leave England? He had a good career there, in a successful firm. He owns shares in it and was making a fortune.'

'But he'll do even better by setting up here,' Hope pointed out. 'It made sense for them to send him to his own country.'

'I don't like things that are too sensible,' her husband complained. 'There's something else behind it.'

Hope nodded. 'I think so, too,' she conceded. 'I just hope it isn't—'

'What?' Toni asked, laying his hand over hers.

'He used to tell us so much about Celia. Every phone call, every letter was all about her. I was surprised when he said she was blind, because he's not a man who— Well—'

'Yes, I can't imagine him living with a woman he has to care for all the time,' Toni agreed. 'But I thought we were wrong. I was proud of him. He even sent us photographs of her, and called her his English rose. I'd never known him to be so committed to a woman before.'

'Then suddenly it's all over,' Hope said, 'and he comes home without her. He's been back for three months now, and he never speaks of her. Why?'

'What are you afraid of?'

'That he left her because his love wasn't great enough for him to cope. I should be sorry to think that was true of any son of mine.'

'But you didn't like him living with her at the start,' Toni pointed out. 'You said her blindness would hold him back.'

She made a face.

'All right, I admit I'm not consistent,' she conceded. 'Is anyone?'

'Never, in all the years I've known you, have you been consistent,' her husband said fondly.

'I wanted him to be sensible.' she said, 'But I suppose I don't like him to be too sensible. I wanted to believe that my son is better than myself, kinder and more generous.'

'Nobody is more generous than you,' Toni protested. 'But for the generosity of your love my life would be nothing.'

'You praise me too much,' she said with a little smile. 'It isn't generous to love a man who gives you everything you want.'

He returned the smile, and she kissed him, but they both knew that it wasn't really true. Despite his love, he didn't give her everything she wanted. Only one man could have done that, and Toni was not that man. It would have been too much to say that he knew it, but he'd always had a suspicion, which he proved by determinedly refusing to ask questions.

Thirty-five years ago he had met Hope, an Englishwoman visiting Italy, a divorcee with three sons: Luke, adopted; Francesco, born during her marriage, but not by her husband; and Primo, the stepson she'd come to love. Toni had loved her from the first moment, and had been overjoyed when she'd agreed to marry him. Only his own children could increase his happiness, and that had come about the following year, with the birth of twin sons, Carlo and Ruggiero.

Since then he had sometimes wondered if Francesco was her secret favourite, but her adoration of each one of her sons was so all-encompassing that it was hard for Toni to be sure of his suspicions. Nor did he ever allow himself to brood about them.

Hope had missed Francesco badly since he'd left home to work in America, later moving to England, but she would have missed any of them who vanished for years, making only brief visits home.

But suddenly, three months ago, he'd returned to Naples from England, ostensibly for his brother's wedding, and full of plans for setting up a branch of his firm and increasing his already healthy fortune. While he looked for somewhere to live he'd moved back into the Villa Rinucci, in the room that had always been kept for him, even when it had seemed he would never occupy it again.

But he had come without the woman he'd once seemed to love, and he would never speak of her.

'You're afraid he just dumped her because she was a burden, aren't you?' Toni asked his wife gently. 'But I don't believe that. Not our Francesco.'

'I've told myself that many times.' Hope sighed. 'But how well do we know him these days?'

'Maybe she dumped him?' Toni suggested mildly.

'Toni, *caro,* you're talking nonsense. A girl with a disability dumping a man who could look after her? No, it's something else—something that gives him bad dreams.'

'He tells you this?' Toni asked, startled.

'No, but sometimes he mutters in his sleep. I've heard him through the door. Last night I heard him cry, "Get out!" At other times he gets up and walks the floor for hours, as though he was afraid to go back to sleep.'

'Now it is you who are talking nonsense,' he told her firmly. 'If he walks the floor, surely it's because he's making plans for the factory? Why should he be afraid to sleep?'

'I wish he would tell me,' Hope said sadly. 'There is something about this situation that he's keeping a secret, and it hurts him.'

'Does he know that you heard him last night?'

'No, I meant to knock on his door, but I lacked the courage.'

'Don't tell me that you're afraid of your own son?' he said in a rallying voice.

'Not exactly. But there's a distant place inside himself, where nobody else is allowed.'

'That's always been there,' Toni pointed out. 'As long as I've known Francesco he's protected that inner place—sometimes fiercely. I remember the very first day we met. He was three years old, and the wary look was already in his eyes.'

'Perhaps he was just nervous at meeting a stranger?' Hope mused.

'Francesco has never been nervous of anyone in his life. People are nervous of him. He's always kept himself to himself. That way he doesn't have to bother with anyone who doesn't interest him.'

'*Caro,* what a cruel thing to say!' Hope protested.

'I don't mean to be cruel, but he's the man he is. He isn't wide-open to people, and his heart is difficult to reach. He prefers it like that. It saves having to make small talk. He's impatient with small talk. It's a waste of time. He told me so.

'You make him sound so grim,' Hope objected.

'He is grim in many ways. He lacks charm, and that's another thing he's glad of.'

'I've always found him very charming,' Hope said, offended.

'So have I. Inside this family he can be delightful. To those he loves he shows warmth and generosity, but to them only. Generally he's indifferent to the world and its opinions, and nothing's going to change him. That's why if this young woman really was the right one, breaking up with her was a greater tragedy than it would be with other men.'

'But *he* dismissed *her.*'

'Did he? I wonder. What a pity you didn't manage to talk to him when you heard him call out in his sleep. He might have opened up at that moment.'

'You're right.' She sighed. 'I'm afraid I've missed the chance. This morning he rose early and left before the rest of us were up.'

'Careful to avoid us,' Toni murmured.

'No, no, I'm sure we're making too much of this, and all is well with him,' she said, as lightly as she could manage.

Toni rested his hand fondly on her shoulder.

'If you say so, *carissima,*' he said.

For the rest of the day Hope was inwardly disturbed. The

conversation of the morning haunted her, and she found herself repeatedly going out onto the terrace to look down the path to where a car would climb the hill, hoping that Francesco would return early.

But there was no sign of him, and at last the light began to fade.

Despondently, she was about to go inside but stopped at the sight of something moving on the road below. A vehicle was climbing the hill, and for a moment she allowed herself to hope. But then she saw that it was a taxi. It stopped at the steps and the driver got out to open the rear passenger door.

The first creature out was a dog, a beautiful black Labrador, wearing the harness of a guide dog. A strange feeling came over Hope, and she began to understand even before she saw the other occupant unfold her long, graceful legs and step out. It was the young woman in the pictures Francesco had sent her.

'Good afternoon,' Hope called, speaking her native English. 'You must be Signorina Ryland.'

Celia paid the driver, who set a bag beside her, offering to take it into the house. She declined, gracefully, and he drove away. Her face, turned to Hope's, was bright and smiling.

'*Buongiorno,*' she said. '*Si, sono la Signorina Ryland. E penso che siate la Signora Rinucci.*'

Hope was both charmed and impressed by this young woman who confirmed her own identity and guessed that of her hostess in excellent Italian. Then Celia added, 'But if you are Francesco's mother, you're as English as I am, or so he's told me.'

'Indeed, I am,' Hope confirmed.

She reached out to shake Celia's hand, taking the opportunity to assess her, and had the disconcerting impression that she was being assessed in return.

She knew it was false. Celia's eyes were sightless, but it

was impossible to tell—not merely because they were large and beautiful, of an incredibly clear blue, but also because they were full of life. Mysteriously, they contrived to be both guileless and shrewd.

'I'm glad we've met at last,' Hope said. 'It was time. Come inside. Can I take your bag?'

'Thank you, but I can carry it.'

'Then let's go in. There are five broad steps just in front of you.'

'If you walk ahead, Jacko will follow you.'

The Labrador did so, finding the way after Hope until they were in the large living room and Celia was sitting. Then he curled up unobtrusively close to her chair.

'Perhaps he would like some water?' Hope suggested.

'He'd love some,' Celia said quickly. 'He works so hard.'

In a few moments Jacko was gulping down water, making so much noise that Celia smiled, reaching down to touch him lightly.

Hope took the chance to study her, and was astonished by what she saw. Unconsciously she'd fallen victim to the assumption that blind meant dowdy. Now she saw how wrong she'd been. This self-assured young woman made no concessions to her disability. She was dressed with a combination of elegance and daring that actually suggested hours in front of a mirror, getting every detail right.

Her hair was a flamboyant red, just muted enough to be natural, just adventurous enough to be a statement. For the life of her Hope couldn't decide which.

Her make-up was discreetly flawless, her pale complexion offset by a delicate rose tint in her cheeks. Her figure was magnificent, encased in a deep blue trouser suit whose close fit and superb tailoring managed to be both demure and revealing.

The thought flitted across Hope's mind: *If my son threw her away, he's a fool.*

'Francesco didn't tell me that you were coming,' Hope said. 'If he had, I would have looked forward to it.'

'He doesn't know I'm in Naples. I came to return some of his property. When he left our apartment in London he was in a hurry, and he left things behind.'

'And you've come all the way to Naples to return them to him?' Hope asked.

'No, I was coming, anyway. I work here now. It seemed a good idea to bring them myself.'

A thousand questions rose to Hope's lips. She wanted to ask Celia all about herself and Francesco, and what had happened between them, but she found that something forced the questions back. This young woman had a simple dignity that was impressive.

At Hope's request she talked about the work that had brought her here. She spoke with enthusiasm but no self-pity, and laughter seemed to come naturally to her.

Hope's first thought had been that Celia wanted to reclaim Francesco. Now she wasn't so sure. This was a strong, independent girl, and Hope couldn't believe she'd come to get her claws into him. She didn't need him. She didn't need anyone.

'Let's have some fresh coffee,' she said at last, rising. 'I'll just go into the kitchen and tell Rosa. She's the best cook in Naples—but you'll discover that for yourself when you come to dinner.'

'Thank you. I'd love to.'

Hope was gone a few minutes. Just as she prepared to return she heard the sound of a car drawing up outside, and a glance out of the window showed her Francesco arriving. She was about to call him when she realised Celia would be bound to hear her. Instead, she returned to the main room, and arrived just a second too late.

Francesco had started to walk through the doorway when he saw Celia. He stopped dead, silent and motionless. Hope, watching his face from the other side of the room, saw in it all she wanted to know.

The sight of her had astounded him, penetrating his armour that was so strong against the rest of the world, leaving him exposed and defenceless. He just stood there, staring at Celia, paler than his mother had ever seen him before. He actually seemed unable to speak, and his breathing was shallow, as though he'd received a blow over the heart.

'Hallo, Francesco,' Celia said calmly.

Of course she recognised him, Hope thought. She knew his step. Of the two of them, she was the one in command of this situation.

Although she had spoken to Francesco, Celia's face was half turned away from him, so that Hope had a good view of her expression and saw the soft, eager smile that touched her mouth. Her eyes danced with pure joy.

'I had no idea that you were coming to Italy,' Francesco said slowly, and there was a slight hesitation in his voice that would have been a stammer in any other man.

'I thought it was time I changed my life,' she said cheerfully. 'Found new horizons, learned new skills.'

'But—why Italy?'

'Because you may recall that I spent some time learning Italian in case you and I ever came here together. It seemed a shame to waste it. So if you had any idea that I'd come trotting after you, you can just think again, oh, conceited one!'

'That wasn't what I—'

'Yes, it was. It's the first thing that came into your head.'

'Well, I didn't expect to find you sitting in my mother's front room. Does she know who you are?'

'I think she guessed as soon as she saw Jacko.'

'Who the hell is Jacko? Your latest romance?'

'You might say we're constantly in each other's company. He takes me everywhere.'

'I'll bet he never gets told to keep his hands to himself because you're better off without him,' Francesco said bitterly.

Celia's voice rose slightly in indignation.

'For pity's sake, Jacko is my *dog!*'

He swore under his breath.

'Don't be vulgar, my son,' Hope said.

'I didn't see you there, Mamma. This is—yes—well…' His voice trailed off as he realised the incongruity of what he was saying.

'I've been here over an hour,' Celia said merrily. 'Your mother knows who I am by now. I came to return some things that belong to you. They're in that bag by my feet, next to Jacko.'

'He's black,' Francesco said, regarding Jacko. 'I didn't see him in the shadow.'

'Come and say hallo to him,' Celia offered.

He came forward uneasily and reached out to stroke the dog, who stretched up his head for a moment, then settled down again. Francesco seated himself close enough to Celia to talk quietly.

'I don't believe this is happening. What the devil are you doing here?'

'I've told you. But well done for being honest! None of that stuff about pretending to be glad to see me.'

He bit his lip. So often in the past he'd snagged himself on her sharp wits, and clearly nothing had changed.

'Is there any reason why I should be glad to see you?' he growled.

'None that I can think of.'

'Good. Then, as you say, honesty is the best policy.'

'I expect you've got someone else by now,' she said casually. 'Don't worry, I'm not here to make trouble.'

'There's no—' He checked himself but it was too late. Now she would know.

'Then I'm not causing you any problems by being here?' she said.

'No problem at all,' he agreed briskly. 'I'm glad to see that you seem to be on top of the world.'

'Right on top,' she agreed. 'I love your country.'

She repeated the last words in Italian, for the benefit of Hope, whose footsteps she could hear. Delighted, Hope explained in Italian that her husband was here, too, and introduced him.

Celia responded with a few more words in Italian, which made Toni tease, 'Ah, but can you speak our dialect?'

He proceeded to teach her a few words of Neapolitan, which she mastered at once, and demanded to learn more.

'You learn very fast,' Toni said admiringly. 'I expect you're good at that?'

'Yes, I depend on my mind a lot more than sighted people have to,' Celia said calmly. 'My parents, who are blind, too, used to teach me all sorts of memory tricks when I was a child. I'm still proud of my memory, but, of course, now there are all sorts of gadgets to make life easy.'

'Easy?' Toni echoed, smiling at her kindly. 'Well, perhaps.'

Hope drew Francesco aside.

'I think she's marvellous,' she said. 'What possessed you to leave her?'

'I didn't leave her, Mamma. She threw me out. She actually said, 'I don't want to see you here again.' She *talks* like that—like a sighted person—because she almost doesn't realise that she's any different to anyone else. And I can't make her realise it.'

'Perhaps you're wrong to try,' Hope says thoughtfully. 'Why do you want to force her to realise something she doesn't want to know?'

'Because she can't live for ever in a fantasy. I only wanted her to be a little realistic—'

'Realistic?' Hope echoed, aghast. 'Do you think you have anything to teach that girl about realism? I don't wonder she threw you out. I'd like to do the same.'

'You'll probably get around to it,' he said with a wry grin.

Before she could say any more there was a small buzz from Celia's wrist.

'It's my watch,' she explained. 'I set the alarm to go for six o'clock. I have to get back to town and meet a customer.'

'But I want you to have supper with us,' Hope mourned.

'I'm sorry, I'd have loved to, but I'm still making my mark in a new job, so I have to try to impress people.'

'But you will come another night?' Hope asked anxiously.

'I'll look forward to it. Can you call me a taxi?'

'I'll take you,' Francesco said at once. 'I'll be home later, Mamma.'

'Thank you,' Celia said. 'Jacko?'

Hope saw Francesco lean forward, as though about to take her arm, then check himself and pull his hand back quickly. Something told Hope that Celia was fully aware of this, although she showed no sign of awareness.

'Until we meet again, *signora,*' she said to Hope, before following Jacko out of the door.

CHAPTER FOUR

'WHERE are we going?' he asked as he started up the car.

'It's a little café called the Three Bells.'

'I know it.'

Silence. This was the first time they'd been alone together since the split, and suddenly there was nothing to say. Francesco, taken totally by surprise, was full of confusion.

When he first arrived in Italy he'd been sure she would contact him, but as the silence had stretched out he'd begun to realise that she'd really meant their parting to be permanent.

But *parting* was too light a word for it. Celia hadn't left him, she'd cruelly dismissed him, tossing him out of her home as though desperate to rid herself of all traces of his presence.

Even then he hadn't believed in the finality of what had happened. How could he when their love had been so total, so overwhelming? For him it had been unlike any other love. Transient affairs had come and gone. Women had spoken to him of love and he had repeated the words with, he now knew, only the vaguest understanding of their meaning.

Real love had caught him off-guard, with a young woman who was awkward, provocative, annoying, difficult for the sake of it—it had often seemed to him—unreasonable, stubborn and full of laughter.

Perhaps it was her laughter that had won him. He wasn't a man who laughed often. He understood a good joke, but amusement hadn't formed a major part of his life.

She, on the other hand, would never stop. With so much stacked against her she would collapse with delight at the slightest thing. Often her laughter was aimed at himself, for reasons he could not divine. At first it had been an aggravation, then a delight. Let her laugh at him if she pleased. He was her happy slave. Nothing would have made him admit that to anyone else, but within his heart he had known a flowering.

In her arms he'd become a different man, shedding the tough outer shell like unwanted armour and being passionately grateful to her for making it happen.

He'd known what had happened to him, and had assumed it was the same for her. He'd tried to take reassurance from this, reasoning that the sheer violence of her feelings meant that she was bound to change her mind about their parting. She would calm down, understand that their love was worth fighting for, forgive him whatever he'd done wrong—for he still wasn't quite sure—even perhaps, apologise.

But none of it had happened. She'd been there when he'd cleared out his things from the apartment, had made him a coffee and told him she was sorry it had ended this way. But that was all. The long, heartfelt discussion that should have marked the end of their relationship had simply never happened. Night after night he'd sat by the phone, waiting for her to call and say they must meet just once more, to clear the air. But the phone hadn't rung. He'd sat there for hours, until the silence had eaten into him and he'd been close to despair.

He hadn't called her after that. Not even when he was leaving for Naples. Why bother? It was over.

And now, when he'd just about taught himself to believe that they would never meet again, here she was, tearing up his preconceptions, stranding him in new territory, as awkward and unpredictable as ever. He wanted to bang his head against the steering wheel.

Sitting next to him in the car, Celia tuned in to his agitation and distress. That was easy—because she shared it. She had come to his home knowing she might meet him, thinking herself prepared. She had even congratulated herself on her well-laid plans, but they had all vanished the moment she'd heard his voice. In the surge of joy at being near him again she'd almost forgotten how carefully she had arranged everything, and for a wild moment had almost thrown herself into his arms.

But that would have been a disaster—as she'd recognised when she'd forced herself to calm down. In his arms, in his bed, she would forget the things that had driven them apart—but only for a little while. Soon it would all happen again, and the second parting would be final. At all costs she must prevent that.

She had come to Italy with a set purpose. She would reclaim him, and this time it would be for ever—or never.

Per sempre, she mused, practising her Italian. For ever. *Per sempre e eternità.* And if not—*finita.*

'We're just entering Naples now,' he said at last. 'Have you been to the Three Bells before?'

'Yes, several times. I've got a favourite table in the garden, under the trees.'

As he drew up she said, 'Thank you for the lift. There's no need for me to trouble you any further.'

'Don't speak to me as though I was a stranger,' he growled.

'Let me escort you to the table. I won't try to take your arm. That's a promise.'

He spoke roughly, but she knew him well enough to hear the pain that would have escaped anybody else.

'Don't be silly,' she said, also speaking roughly, to cover the fact that his unhappiness wounded her. 'I'd like you to escort me. Then,' she added, hastily recovering her self-possession, 'I can buy you a drink and show off my Italian.'

'It's a deal.'

He opened the door for her, and there followed an awkward moment when she reached out for his hand, but it wasn't there. Swearing, he lunged forward, trying to put things right, and stumbled over Jacko, who'd got himself into position. Celia instinctively tightened her hand on his, almost saving him from falling.

He swore again, louder this time, and with real fury.

'I'm sorry,' he snapped. 'The hell with everything. I'm sorry.'

'Let's go and sit down,' she said hastily.

He went ahead, followed by Jacko, with Celia walking afterwards. When they were seated at the table under the trees she was as good as her word, speaking to the waiter in Italian and ordering drinks for them both.

'You did that very well,' he conceded when they'd been served.

'You're a good teacher. I took your lessons to heart.'

'Some of them,' he remembered. 'Some you tossed back in my face.'

'Not about Italian.'

'No, just everything else. It got so that everything I said was wrong—'

'Only because you started every sentence with, "I'll do that for you," or "You shouldn't be doing that."'

'And you ended up wanting to kill me,' he remembered. 'I suppose I'm lucky to still be alive.'

'Yes, we were going downhill fairly fast,' she said.

'I'm sorry about what happened at the car. I thought I knew what you wanted, so I didn't reach out my hand to you—'

'But why not? You'd have assisted a sighted woman as a matter of courtesy, wouldn't you? So why not me?'

He drew a slow breath of frustration.

'Excuse me while I bang my head on the tree,' he said at last.

Celia gave a sudden chuckle. 'It's like old times to hear you take that long breath. It always meant that you were clenching and unclenching your hands.'

Goaded, he spoke without thinking. 'I don't know what you'd do with eyes if you had them. You see everything without them.'

She beamed. 'That's the nicest thing you've ever said to me.'

'Now you're confusing me again.'

'It's the first time you've ever made a joke about my eyes,' she explained.

'It wasn't exactly a joke.'

'Pity. I thought you were improving. Anyway, don't apologise about what happened at the car. If we'd both fallen it would have been my fault.'

'Or your new friend's, for moving when I wasn't expecting him to.'

'Don't blame poor Jacko,' Celia protested, instinctively reaching down to caress the dog's head. 'He was only doing his job.'

'But who is he? Last time I saw you, you had Wicksy.'

'Poor Wicksy was getting old, and it wouldn't have been fair to bring him to a strange country. He'd earned a comfortable retirement, and that's what he has. Remember how he liked children? There are three in his new home to make a fuss of him. I went to say goodbye before I came to Italy, and I could tell that he was happy.'

She stopped suddenly.

'What is it?' he asked gently.

'As I left I could hear him playing with the children, barking with excitement, as though he'd forgotten me already. I'm glad of that, truly. I'd hate to think of him pining for me, but he was the best friend I had.'

'And now you're pining for him?' Francesco supplied.

'Yes, I am. We were such a perfect team.'

'Aren't you a perfect team with Jacko?'

'It's too soon to say. His name is short for Giacomo, and he's a real Italian dog. He's always lived in Naples, so he knows it well and I can trust him completely. He even understands the Neapolitan dialect.'

'But how long will you have him? He looks quite elderly, too.'

'He's nine, and he might have retired when his previous owner regained his sight. But I needed a really experienced dog, so they assigned him to me for a while.'

'Then what? Will they give you a younger one?' Francesco asked casually.

Celia shrugged. 'Maybe.'

He understood. Maybe then she would go home. He wished she would go home now.

He wished she would stay for ever.

He wished she had never come here.

The waiter served their drinks, and they sipped in silence for a while.

'You're very quiet,' she said. 'Did I offend you by turning up?'

'Of course not. I'm just a little surprised.'

'You told me so much about Naples I wanted to find out for myself. I used to look forward to coming here with you, and visiting all the places you told me about, seeing if it had all the lovely smells. You were right about that. I walk through the streets here and I can smell the cooking. Mmm!'

'But how did you get here?'

'I went home to my parents for a while, and they said it was time I explored the world a little. Dad gave me a large cheque and told me to blow it on enjoying myself.'

'But you said you have a job here. Aren't you supposed to be just a tourist?'

'I've invested the money. I fancy myself as an entrepreneur. That's how I'm going to enjoy myself. You taught me that.'

'I did?'

'You used to talk a lot about finance. It was your great interest in life. I listened and learned at the master's feet.'

'Is that a way of telling me that money is all I know?'

'Don't be so touchy. You showed me that making money could be fun, so now I'm going to double mine. Or treble it.'

'Or lose it?' he suggested lightly.

'Oh, no, that won't happen,' she assured him.

'How can you be so sure?'

Celia turned her head so that her clear blue eyes were facing him, so full of expression that he could almost swear she saw him.

'Because I never lose,' she said simply. 'When I want something, I make sure I get it.'

'And when you've finished with it you throw it out, marked "No longer needed,"' he said quietly.

'Francesco, do you know how bitter you sound? I wish you wouldn't. We promised each other that we wouldn't be bitter.'

'Did we? I don't remember.'

'The day you came to collect your things,' she reminded him. 'We had a chat then.'

'Oh, yes, it was all very civilised, wasn't it? But I don't remember that we talked things over. Five minutes over coffee and that was that.'

'Well, there wasn't much to talk about, was there?'

'Except you throwing me out.'

'I asked you not to be bitter because I didn't want you to hate me. Still, I guess that wasn't very realistic of me.'

'I don't hate you,' he said gruffly. 'But neither can I pretend that it didn't happen.'

'I don't want to pretend that, either,' she said with a touch of eagerness. 'It did happen, and I'm glad of it. You left me with some of the most wonderful memories I'll ever have, and I want to keep them. Don't you want to?'

'No,' he said with sudden violence. 'I don't want to remember any of it. What use are memories when the reality has gone?'

She gave a little sigh. 'I suppose you're right. We're agreed, then. No memories. We never met before.'

'Why did you come here?' he growled. 'To have a laugh at my expense?'

'No. Why should you say that? Why should I laugh? I can tell you're doing very well without me.'

He shot her a look so fierce that he was actually glad she couldn't see. It was on the tip of his tongue to tell her that she didn't know what she was talking about. Unless, he thought, she'd been trying to provoke him. He only wished he knew.

'Who's your customer?' he asked, for something to say. It was strange how the silences troubled him more than her.

'He's not really a customer. I said that so as not to bore your parents with involved explanations. We work together. His name is Sandro Danzi. He owns a firm organising trips for blind people.'

'Is he blind himself?' he couldn't stop himself asking.

'Does it matter?' she flashed back instinctively.

'For pity's sake! Aren't I even allowed to ask?'

'Why is it always the first thing you ask?'

'It isn't.'

'One of the first. As though nothing else mattered in comparison.'

It mattered, but not in the way she thought. Another blind person understood things that she understood, was potentially closer to her than he could ever be, and that excluded him.

'I didn't mean it like that,' he said, wishing he could find the words to say that he was jealous. Why couldn't she simply understand?

Celia clenched her hands, hating herself. How often had she lashed out at him, wounding him for something that she knew he couldn't help? But she couldn't let down her guard. She didn't dare. It was part of her fight not to be swallowed alive by her blindness, and it seemed the cruelest trick of fate that he should be ranged on the other side.

She sat listening. Even in the bustle of the café she could sense the silence that belonged only to him. She had never seen him, but she knew what he looked like—not the details of his face and body, but the tension of his attitude that told of misery.

'Don't look like that,' she begged.

'How do you know how I look?' he demanded.

'I know your silences,' she said sadly. 'I can always tell.'

Why was she here? she wondered. In a moment of madness she'd thrown up everything and followed him to Naples, hoping to teach him that he could love her and still let her be free. But within a few hours they were enmeshed in the old quarrel. Nothing had changed. However much it hurt, perhaps they were better apart. In a moment she would find the courage to tell him finally.

'Are you hoping for a PR contract from Sandro Danzi?' he asked, in the tone of a man determined to find a more pleasant subject.

'No, I already have that. I've invested my money in his business, and I might go in a bit deeper.'

At Celia's feet Jacko gave a small grunt and became alert.

'What is it, boy?' she asked, touching him gently.

'He's seen another guide dog,' Francesco said.

The strange dog was leading a young man towards them.

'Hey, there!' he called.

'Sandro!' Celia's face lit up. 'This way,' she called.

The newcomer was in his early thirties, tall and strikingly handsome, with a brilliant smile that appeared as soon as he heard her voice.

'Go for it, boy,' he instructed his guide, and the dog came forward confidently until he reached the table, gave Francesco an appraising look, and nudged Celia with his nose.

Francesco rose and stood back while Celia said the stranger's name again, reaching out a hand to him.

'Meet my friend Francesco,' she said. 'Can we talk English? My Italian isn't up to a three-way conversation.'

Sandro put out a hand, which Francesco shook briefly. Sandro's returning clasp was firm and confident, and although he had to reach behind him to find a chair he did so in the easy way of a man with no real doubts.

'Francesco, this is Sandro,' Celia said.

'I'm her boss,' Sandro said at once. 'She does as I tell her.'

'No way!' Celia instantly riposted. 'I'm his associate. I give advice, and he listens if he knows what's good for him.'

Sandro laughed. 'Well, it was worth a try. I'm always trying to get the better of her, but I haven't managed it yet. Awkward, prickly, argumentative, difficult, contrary—did I miss anything?'

'If you did, I'll remind you later,' Celia said through her laughter.

'Tell me, Francesco,' Sandro continued, 'have you found her awkward?'

'Don't get him started on that subject,' Celia said. 'He becomes so annoyed with me that he may go off pop.'

'You have my sympathy,' Sandro observed to Francesco.

'Thank you, but I don't need sympathy,' Francesco said, hearing himself sound pompous and stuffy, hating it, but unable to stop.

'Really? I'd have thought anyone who'd experienced Celia's more maddening ways had earned all the sympathy he could get.'

'Oi!' Celia cried indignantly.

'The world should know the truth.' Sandro sighed. 'I'm black-and-blue from the bruises. At least, they tell me I'm black-and-blue. For all I'd know I could be pink-and-green.'

'Red-and-yellow,' Celia supplied.

'Polka dot!' Sandro declared triumphantly.

Celia loved that, Francesco noted grimly. She laughed and laughed, reaching out to Sandro, touching his arm until he took her hand, and they sat there shaking, united in mirth.

Francesco watched them, feeling lonelier and more excluded than ever in his life.

'I'd better be going,' he said politely. Part of him wanted to escape, but part wanted to say here and watch them.

'Don't let me drive you away,' Sandro said politely. 'Stay for a coffee.'

'Just one, thank you,' Francesco said.

Then he would go, leaving them with each other, and he would never see or think of her again. Meantime, he must make polite conversation.

'So you're in business together?' he said. 'Is it going well?'

'It's getting off the ground,' Celia said.

To Francesco's surprise this remark was greeted with a deep groan. 'You promised…you promised,' Sandro moaned.

'Oh, dear—yes, I did.' She looked overwhelmed with guilt. '*Mea culpa, mea culpa, mea maxima culpa,*' she intoned, beating her breast.

'You're frightening the dogs,' Sandro told her sternly.

'Sorry! Sorry!'

'She swore she wouldn't make any more terrible puns,' Sandro explained to Francesco. 'And that one was *truly* terrible. It was the worst pun I've ever heard. And I've heard them all.'

'Quit boasting!' Celia ordered him.

'Yes, ma'am.'

'But I don't understand,' Francesco said. 'Where was the pun?'

'We've got a little firm called Follia Per Sempre,' Sandro told him. 'Madness For Ever. It used to be mine until my friend here mounted a hostile takeover bid—'

'I bought half,' Celia put in quickly.

'It exists to help blind people,' Sandro resumed.

'You mean, visual aids?' Francesco asked.

'Good Lord, no way. None of that sensible stuff. *Madness* means exactly that—helping the blind do crazy things.'

'The crazier the better,' Celia supplied.

'Like deep-sea diving,' Francesco muttered.

'That, too, and parachuting,' Sandro said cheerfully.

'Parachuting?' Despite his good resolutions Francesco couldn't keep the outrage out of his voice. 'You don't seriously mean jumping out of aircraft and falling thousands of feet?'

'And why not?' Celia asked in a challenging voice.

'Because—' Francesco tried to control himself and failed.

'Because you're *blind,* that's why not. Because it's madness. Because you could be killed.'

'Anyone can be killed,' Celia riposted. 'Why shouldn't we be as free to take the risks as sighted people?'

'You could say that we're acting like a pair of damned fools,' Sandro said, seeming to consider the matter seriously. 'And you'd probably be right. But why not? There are as many sighted fools as blind fools, but we're supposed to keep quiet about our foolishness.'

'We're supposed to keep quiet about a lot of things.' Celia sighed.

'That's true,' Sandro said at once. 'But no more. The days of silence are over. We stand up for our right to act like idiots.'

'Indeed, we do,' added Celia sonorously.

'Plenty of people think like you,' Sandro said, in a voice so reasonable that Francesco wanted to commit murder. 'They feel that blind people should know their place as semi-invalids, and be grateful that the world allows them to emerge into the light at all. Our firm exists to combat that view. The dafter it is, the more we want to do it.'

'You could say,' Celia added, 'that stupidity is a human right, and it ought to be enshrined in law somewhere.'

'Why bother?' Francesco said crossly. 'You're doing fine without the law.'

'Celia, I think your friend is afflicted with a severe case of common sense,' Sandro said, shaking his head.

'I know,' she replied mournfully. 'I've been trying to cure him, but I'm afraid it's too late.'

'But our fight continues?'

'Indeed, it does. Never let it be said that we were deterred by common sense!'

'Will you two stop?' Francesco said, goaded beyond endurance. 'People are looking at you.'

'That's all right,' Sandro said cheerily. 'We can't see them, so it doesn't bother us.'

It was the way they both said *we* that pierced Francesco like a knife. *We*—we who live in a world from which you are excluded.

'I'll leave you two to talk business,' he said, rising.

'Actually, we're leaving, too,' Celia said. 'Did you bring the stuff?' This was to Sandro.

'All of it.'

'Then we'll listen to it on my machine at home.'

'Let me drive you there,' Francesco said.

Courtesy demanded that he make the offer, but it tore him apart. On the one hand it would tell him where she lived. On the other it would force him to deliver her there with another man, and then drive away while they went in together.

When they were in the car Celia said, 'I live in the Via Santa Lucia. That's near the shore.'

'The quickest way from here—' Sandro began, and proceeded to give every turning accurately.

'You know the way very well,' Francesco said through gritted teeth.

'That's because I used to live there. I designed the interior to suit my needs, and when Celia needed somewhere, and I'd already moved out—'

'Yes, I understand,' Francesco said hastily.

Before long he was drawing up outside a tall apartment block.

'Thanks, we'll manage from here,' Sandro said. 'It's only on the lowest floor. Good evening.'

Francesco replied politely and stayed in the car, watching them go in. He could see the apartment. The only one in the building that was dark. He sat for a moment, waiting for the lights to go on, until it dawned on him that this wouldn't happen. The two inside had no need of lights. United in confidence and laughter, they were also united in their indifference to darkness.

He pictured them going inside, turning on the computer, listening together, deep in their private world

Sandro would say, *Who on earth was that?*

And she would reply, *Oh, that's just Francesco. He's nobody. I thought he was getting a bit tense.*

He's always tense about something. Forget him!

And they would.

After a while he drove away.

CHAPTER FIVE

'I'VE decided to invite Celia to have dinner with the family,' Hope declared three days later. 'I would like to know her better.'

Francesco forced himself to smile.

'That's nice of you, Mamma, but I don't think she'll accept.'

'Why ever not? She likes going out. She told me so. Anyway, she's already accepted. I noted her cellphone number when she was here, and called her last night.'

Francesco had the feeling that a tank was rolling over him. It was a sensation familiar to all Hope's sons, but for once he tried to rebel.

'Mamma—'

'She agreed in principle, but we still have to set a date. Kindly ask her if Saturday would suit, or if she would prefer another date.'

'Why don't you do that yourself, since you get on so well?'

'Because I want her to understand that the invitation comes from you also. Besides, surely you know her better than I?'

'I'm not sure,' he said wryly.

'Oh, you're being difficult today. Very well, I'll send her an e-mail.'

'You have her e-mail address?'

'Oh, yes, and she told me how it works. When she opens her e-mails the computer turns them to speech. She listens, then replies into the microphone, and it reaches me in the normal way. Didn't you know that?'

'Yes, I knew that. I just didn't realise you and she had exchanged so much information.'

'You'd be amazed at how much I know, my son.' Then, seeing his darkened eyes, she added gently, 'But Celia was also discreet about many things.'

He relaxed slightly.

His first thought had been to rebel against this dinner invitation. He'd had no sign of Celia since the day she'd visited the villa. He hadn't contacted her, and although he braced himself whenever the phone rang it was never her.

Now he was becoming used to the situation, and he told himself that his mother's idea might be a good one, establishing for both of them that they could still be friends, in a civilised manner.

Besides, he missed her damnably.

Celia accepted for Saturday, and the word went out to as many of the family as could make it. Primo and Olympia accepted at once, so did Carlo and his wife, Della, and also Ruggiero, whose marriage to Polly three months earlier had provided Francesco with his excuse for a sudden return. Luke and his wife, Minnie, made a special trip from Rome.

Only Justin was missing—Hope's eldest son, who lived in England with his wife and three children. But in a phone call he promised to bring his whole family 'for the wedding.' Francesco had spent so much time abroad that his love-life had been a closed book to them for too long. Now everyone was curious about his lady.

'Giulio and Teresa are coming,' Toni informed Hope,

mentioning his elder brother and his wife, who lived just outside Naples.

'Excellent.'

'Also Teresa's sister, Angelica,' Toni said, in the tone of one making a confession. '*Cara,* I know you don't like her—'

'I don't dislike her. I just wish she'd shut up sometimes and let someone else speak,' Hope said frankly. 'And she's horribly tactless.'

'I know, but she's visiting them just now, so she had to be included.'

'You'll have to take care of her, Poppa,' said Carlo, who happened to be there at that moment. 'Keep her attention occupied.'

'How?' Toni demanded plaintively.

'You must flirt with her,' Hope declared calmly. 'She's quite attractive for her age, so you should have no trouble.'

'You wouldn't mind my flirting with her?' Toni asked his wife faintly.

'We must all do whatever is necessary, *caro.*'

She kissed him and departed from the breakfast table, humming, leaving her menfolk aghast.

'You'll have to take firm action, Poppa,' Francesco said, grinning.

'How?' his much-tried father repeated.

'Strike a blow for all men. *Really* flirt with Aunt Angelica. Make Mamma so jealous that she'll be careful what she tells you to do in future.'

'But my heart wouldn't be in it.' Toni sighed. 'And your mother knows that.'

'Of course, or she'd never have suggested it,' Carlo said. 'She knows she's got you on a string.'

Toni nodded. 'Always,' he said. 'Right from the moment I first set eyes on her.'

On Friday Hope informed Francesco that he was to collect Celia the next day and bring her to the villa.

'Perhaps she'd rather get here without my help,' he observed.

'No, she's fine about that,' Hope informed him. 'She said she'd prefer you to a taxi.'

'I see that the two of you have decided everything,' he observed.

'Of course. No point in waiting for you. Make sure you look your best tomorrow.'

'Any minute you'll be telling me to wash behind my ears,' he said wrathfully.

'Don't forget to do that, either,' Hope instructed him.

He might complain that his mother still treated him like a kid, but the next day he was on the road to Celia's apartment, elegantly turned out and wondering what kind of reception he would receive. Whatever it was, he decided that his best course was to keep back emotionally and stay safe. Somehow he would endure the evening, although he couldn't think how.

Celia was sitting by the window as he drew the car up, her head turned slightly in an attitude of listening. By the time he reached the door she was already opening it.

She was beautiful, in a long dress of honey-coloured silk which brought out the soft glow of her skin and the blue of her eyes. Diamonds sparkled in her ears and about her neck. They were tiny. It was Celia's way never to overdo things. But they announced that she was putting the flags out tonight.

'You're lovely,' he said, instantly forgetting his resolution to be distant.

'Will I do you credit?'

'You don't need to ask that. You know exactly what you look like. Don't ask me how, but you do know.'

She laughed delightedly. 'Yes, I do. I chose this colour because I know you like it.'

'Well, I guess you know my tastes well enough by now to be able to pick the colours in the— *Hell!*' He caught himself up, horrified at what he'd nearly said.

Had there ever been another woman like this one? he wondered. Celia laughed and laughed until he thought she would collapse.

'In the dark!' she choked. 'You were going to say in the *dark.*'

'All right, I'm sorry,' he growled. 'I forgot—'

'Of course you did. Oh, darling, that's wonderful. I begin to think you're human after all.'

He stared at her, feeling all at sea—not for the first time.

'You're not upset? I didn't mean to—'

'I know. You didn't mean to make a joke about my blindness but you did—well, you almost did. It's a start. I'll teach you yet.'

'Will I ever understand you?'

'Probably not. Never mind. Give me a kiss.'

He opened his arms and would have drawn her against him, but she brushed her lips faintly against his and slipped away at once. He followed into her front room, where a dark gold velvet jacket lay over a chair. Beside it sat Jacko, wearing his harness.

'Ready?' she asked him, reaching for the jacket.

'We don't need to take him, surely?' Francesco asked, taking the jacket and holding it up to receive her arms. 'I'll be with you all the time.'

'I can't leave him behind,' she said firmly. 'It would be like telling him he's useless when he needs reassurance. He hasn't quite settled with me yet. Jacko!'

The dog came to stand obediently in front of her.

'*Andiamo!*' she said.

As soon as he heard the Italian for *let's go!* Jacko turned so that she could take hold of the long handle.

'We're ready,' Celia said. 'If you'll just open the door and lead the way?'

He did so, escorting them to the car, showing Jacko into the back and Celia into the front.

'I'd better warn you that there's going to be a big crowd tonight,' he said. 'My family all want to meet you. Including,' he added in a hollow voice, 'Aunt Angelica.'

'Is she the one who puts her foot in it?'

'Good grief, you mean, I've told you about her before?'

'Not at all,' Celia reassured him. 'But every family has one.'

'Well, you're right—she's ours.'

She gave a chuckle. 'I'll remember.'

Everyone was waiting when the car pulled up at the villa. They stood on the terrace, watching as Celia climbed the steps, guided by Jacko, but holding Francesco's arm on the other side. One of the men—nobody was ever quite sure which—gave an appreciative wolf whistle, and Celia beamed in equal appreciation.

Uncle Giulio and Aunt Teresa were introduced. Then came Aunt Angelica, full of words, most of them inappropriate.

'I've heard so much about you—all exaggerated, I'm sure. But there, that can't be helped, can it?'

'Can't it?' Celia asked.

'Well, people don't understand, do they? But I pride myself on realising things that are hidden from the rest of the world.'

'Let's start the evening with a glass of wine,' Hope said quickly, appearing with a tray of glasses. 'Celia, *cara,* what would you like to drink?' She named two excellent wines, one white, one red.

'Oh, do have the white!' Angelica exclaimed at once. 'Then if you should spill it on that lovely dress it won't stain. These things happen so easily, but I assure you we'll all understand. You and I must have a nice little talk—'

There was a swift intake of breath from the family, and Francesco cast a horrified glance at Celia. She had pressed her lips tightly together, as though controlling some response or other, but exactly what it was impossible to say.

'But you promised to talk to *me*,' Toni hurried to tell Angelica. 'I'd counted on having all your attention.'

He put an arm firmly around her waist, swept her off as gallantly as a young man, pressed a glass of wine into her hand, and everyone breathed again.

'What's happening now?' Celia asked Francesco.

'Poppa's flirting madly with Aunt Angelica, gazing deep into her eyes until she forgets everything but him, so she won't drop any clangers—for a while, anyway.'

'Doesn't your mother mind him doing that?'

'Mind? She told him to.'

Celia chuckled. 'I knew I was going to like your mother.'

'It's mutual,' Hope assured her. 'What wine would you like?'

'White,' Celia said at once. 'Just in case I have an accident, you know.'

'Nonsense!' Hope said robustly. 'I don't suppose you can remember the last time you had an accident.'

'I do believe you're right,' Celia replied impishly, and everyone relaxed.

From the first moment she was a great success. Her beauty, her merry laugh, her complete ease with who and what she was won everyone over. Standing back a little, Francesco knew a glow of pride in her accomplishments and her courage. They were regarding him with envy, he realised: the man who had won the prize.

If only they knew how far away from the prize he really was!

At his mother's command he had racked his brain to recall Celia's favourite dishes, and now they were served up with a flourish that made it clear she was the guest of honour. She obviously understood and enjoyed this, for she tried everything set before her and was unstinting in her praise.

They admired her for her proficiency in Italian, and competed to teach her words from the Neapolitan dialect.

'All the best words come from Napoli,' Primo told her. 'Take *sfizio*! Only Naples could have produced that word.'

'But I thought that was Italian,' Celia objected. 'It's one of my favourite words.'

'You know what it means, then?' Primo asked with a grin.

'It's the pleasure you get from doing something for the sheer, beautiful, stupid sake of it,' Celia replied, in a voice that held a touch of ecstasy.

Francesco saw his family exchange glances of pleasure, sharing the same thought. If she knew that, she belonged among them.

'It's not really Italian,' Carlo explained. 'It's a Neapolitan word that the rest of the country hijacked because they don't have a word that describes that feeling. You have to be one of us to understand.'

Primo said, 'Francesco must have taught you well for you know about *sfizio*.'

Now they were all regarding Francesco with approval, and he felt awkward—for he hadn't taught her that word. He hadn't even known she knew it. She must have concealed her discovery, knowing that, of all things, it was her love of *sfizio* that he feared most. It had driven her to dive in deep water. It had driven her to cast him out of her life.

But Celia was mistress of the situation.

'I think the English hijacked it, as well,' she said. 'Think of the English word *fizzy*. It means bubbling and sparkling, and if you were *sfizio* you'd probably feel fizzy.' She reached for her wineglass, located it at once and raised it in salute.

'All the best words started in Naples,' she cried.

'*Si*,' they all answered with one voice.

'So here's to being fizzy. May life have an endless supply of fizz.'

They all raised their glasses and joined the toast. Francesco did the same, but only so that they wouldn't notice how uneasy he was.

The meal over, they went into the next room, which led onto the terrace. With the doors wide-open and the huge windows pulled back, the party could spill out into the night air.

Celia was enthroned on the sofa, and it seemed to Francesco that people were queuing up to speak to her.

'She's touting for business,' Primo said with a grin. He owned a factory in Naples which Olympia, his wife, ran for him. It was Olympia who sat head to head with Celia now.

'They're discussing modifications to be made so that we can employ more partially sighted people,' Primo said. 'I only overheard a little. I fled when it began to sound expensive.'

As they neared, Olympia hailed them.

'Celia's agreed to come to the factory and suggest some improvements so that we can draw our employees from a wider source,' she said. 'I thought tomorrow would be a good day.'

'That's—that's excellent,' Primo said.

Celia laughed. 'Don't worry. It won't cost as much as

you're afraid of. And you can tell everyone that I'm efficient and not expensive, so I'll get plenty more business.'

'You can have mine,' Francesco said suddenly. 'The factory's just starting up, so we ought to begin as we mean to go on. When you've finished with Olympia perhaps you'd fit me into your diary somewhere?'

'Certainly,' she said, and immediately dictated a brief message into a small recording machine.

'That's what I call style,' Carlo observed. He'd been watching the whole performance with admiration. 'You've been keeping her a secret, Francesco,' he said, in a low voice so that only the two of them could hear.

'You've all got the wrong end of the stick,' Francesco replied in the same voice. 'We're friends, no more. Until recently we hadn't seen each other for months.'

'But you're back together now? Hmm!'

'*Mio dio!* You're as bad as Mamma.'

'Nobody's as bad as Mamma,' Carlo said with feeling.

'Some more wine?' Hope asked, tapping him on the shoulder.

'Mamma—fancy you being there!' Carlo exclaimed, the picture of innocence. 'I had no idea.'

'Indeed! Well, the last time I believed anything you said you were six. Or was it five?'

'Four?' Carlo said helpfully.

'Anyway, don't start planning the wedding, either of you,' Francesco said firmly.

Carlo gave him a humorously jeering look, but it faded when he saw his brother's set expression.

'*Like he'd woken up to find himself in a dungeon,*' he told his brothers later.

From somewhere behind them they heard Angelica's shrill

laugh—only now it had an extra unfortunate edge. Toni was making his way nervously towards them.

'How much wine has she drunk?' Hope asked him.

'It was the only way I could obey you and keep her occupied,' Toni pleaded.

'I said flirt with her, not ply her with drink.' Then a sweet reminiscent smile came over Hope's face. 'You didn't always need wine to turn a woman's head.'

'That was different, *carissima*,' he said. 'That was you.'

The others watched them fondly, delighted by this sudden flicker of late romance as only a family could be. But the spell was soon broken.

'Angelica's coming this way!' Francesco said, aghast.

Clearly emergency action was called for. Carlo dived for the music centre, and in another moment music filled the air.

'Let's dance,' he said, seeing Della, his wife, nearby, and taking her in his arms.

'Let's dance,' Toni said, turning to his wife.

'Is anyone dancing with me?' Celia asked.

'Yes, I am,' Francesco said, drawing her to her feet. 'Before anyone else gets near you.'

'What was going on there?' she demanded, smiling as they moved slowly around the floor. 'The air was thrumming.'

'How much did you hear?' he asked, wondering if she'd heard the remarks about weddings.

'It started with a laugh in the background that could have cracked glass.'

'Aunt Angelica. She's a bit squiffy because Poppa's been plying her with wine.'

'Did your mother tell him to do that, as well as flirt?'

'No, I think he was just running out of ideas. He doesn't

care about anyone but Mamma, so making eyes at another woman comes very hard to him.'

'She must be very sure of him.'

'Totally sure. I don't think he even knows other women exist.'

'How charming!'

'Yes, it's lovely to see a couple so devoted at their age. They'll be celebrating their thirty-fifth wedding anniversary soon.'

'Let me try to get this straight. You're not Toni's son, are you?'

'No, Mamma already had me before she met him.'

'So your father was her first husband?'

'It's a bit complicated. Hold on to me tight, because I'm going to move fast. Angelica's headed for us.'

He turned sharply and managed to spin her the length of the room, out of danger. Celia clung to him, loving every minute and distracted from the way he'd changed the subject—as he had meant her to be.

'Safe now?' she teased as they slowed.

'Quite safe,' he said.

It wasn't really true. He'd spun out of one kind of danger right into another. This had been a mistake. His resolve to hold himself aloof was being set at naught by the closeness of her body and the warm perfume wafting from her.

Memories of a hundred nights came back to him: pure, vigorous sex for the sake of it, love spiced with exquisite tenderness, sometimes one followed by the other. The silk dress might not have been there for all the protection it gave her from his fevered thoughts.

'Am I a credit to you?' she asked lightly. 'I did my best.'

'You look glorious, but—'

'What is it?' She'd felt him stiffen.

'Are you wearing anything under this dress?'

'Of course not. It's tight-fitting satin. I wouldn't want any awkward lines showing.'

He took a deep, ragged breath. 'I'd forgotten what a shocking flirt you are.'

'You don't really mean *flirt*. You mean something much more extreme.'

'Whatever I meant, you're driving me crazy.'

'Of course. It's one of the great pleasures of life. You wouldn't expect me to give it up, would you?'

'You'll never give up any chance to torment me,' he growled. 'I know that.'

'I never tormented you—not on purpose.'

'Are you saying you didn't realise you were doing it? I find that hard to believe.'

'Does that mean you're doubting my word?' she asked lightly.

'It means I know you. You could always tell what was going on, whether you seemed to or not. That was the joke you always had at my expense.'

'But I couldn't always tell,' she mused. 'When we were together there were times when you might have been exchanging lingering glances with every girl in the room. How would I have known?'

'You'd have known,' he said softly. 'Because my attention was always on you, every second of every minute of every day, and you'd have sensed the moment it was taken away. But you knew it never would be. Didn't you?'

'Yes.' She sighed. 'I did know.'

'It was one of the things about me that you found unendurable, wasn't it?'

'Don't say that,' she urged quickly. '*Unendurable* is a terrible word.'

He wanted to say that it described his life without her, but he controlled himself, refusing to admit the truth. He still had his dignity.

But it was hard to think of dignity—or at least to think that it mattered—when the feel of her body gliding against him reminded him of a hundred lovings. Why had she come here to torture him?

'What do you look like?' she whispered. 'If I could see, what would I find in your eyes?'

'The same look that's always been there,' he said softly. 'You never really doubted that, did you?'

'I don't know. Everything became so confused. You gave me so much. It's just that—'

'I gave the wrong things.' With a sudden rush of sadness he added, 'And I always would, wouldn't I? A man can't change himself that much—'

'Don't, Francesco. I didn't mean—'

'Celia, my dear girl!'

Angelica was descending on them, full of a booming bonhomie that would not be denied. She enveloped Celia in a vast bear hug, while Francesco gave an inner groan, knowing how she would hate this.

'I've been searching for you all evening for our get-together,' Angelica informed the world. 'I've been watching you, and I want to tell you how much I admire you. I just can't believe how well you manage to cope with life.'

There was a brief silence. Francesco clenched his hands, knowing that this was the worst thing to say to Celia. Even the others, who didn't know her so well, picked up the tension.

'But what is there to cope with?' Celia asked, smiling. 'I live life just as you do.'

'Not exactly, surely?' Angelica cooed. 'There must be so many things you don't know about—'

'And many things she knows about that we don't,' Francesco said. 'Celia's world is different to ours, but not worse.'

'But surely,' Angelica persisted, 'it must make life very difficult, having so much less than other people—'

Hope and Toni exchanged alarmed glances, but it was Celia who saved the situation by bursting into laughter. Someone suggested more coffee and there was a cheer. Toni took over Angelica again, demanding that she come out and see the stars with him.

'Phew!' Francesco breathed close to Celia's ear.

'She didn't mean any harm,' Celia said, still laughing.

'If I'd said anything like that you'd have hung me out to dry,' he said wryly.

'But you don't say things like that any more. And thank you for what you did say.'

'Well, as you said earlier, I guess I'm learning,' he said lightly.

She turned her face to him with an odd expression, as though she was thinking something important. Suddenly his heart was beating with hope.

But before she could speak they heard the sound of her cellphone coming from inside her bag.

'I'm sorry. I should have turned it off,' she said, hastily reaching for it.

'No problem. We'll leave you in peace,' Hope said.

She shooed everyone away, including Francesco, although he lingered long enough to hear Celia say, '*Ciao,* Sandro.'

He could have cursed. Just when things were going well that *buffone* had to intrude.

'Come away,' Hope said, chivvying him. 'Let her be private.'

'There's no need,' Celia said quickly. 'I'll just tell him I can't talk now.'

She did so, shutting off the phone almost at once, but, still,

Hope drew Francesco away some distance to ask furiously, 'What were you thinking of to let that wonderful creature slip through your fingers?'

'It wasn't quite like that, Mamma.'

'That's a matter of opinion. And who is Sandro?'

'A vulgar nobody,' Francesco snapped, 'who pushes in where he isn't wanted.'

'I see,' Hope mused. 'As dangerous as that?'

CHAPTER SIX

IT WAS A fine evening, and they were both feeling cheerful as they drove away. Francesco's good humour had been restored by Celia's refusal to talk to Sandro for more than a moment.

'Oh, I like your family so much,' she enthused now.

'They just love you. My brothers are particularly impressed with the way you combine pleasure with business.'

'Not just your brothers. I had a most interesting conversation with Olympia who, I gather, is the real power in that factory.'

'Yes, I think Primo has only just discovered that. Jacko was a big success, too. Everyone wanted to make a fuss of him.'

'I know,' Celia said. 'They were all very nice, and asked me first if it was all right to pet him while he was "on duty". I said it was, but I don't think he enjoyed it much. He didn't seem to respond.'

'Not like Wicksy,' Francesco recalled. 'He was a real party animal. But Jacko's always a bit quiet.'

'He and I need a little more time to get used to each other,' Celia said. 'I'm going to give him lots of extra love until he feels better.'

Suddenly she began to chuckle.

'What is it?' he asked, grinning with delight in her pleasure.

'There was one moment tonight when I really wished I had

eyes. It was when Toni announced that he wanted a divorce so that he could marry Angelica.'

Francesco shouted with laughter.

'But he made sure Angelica was safely off the premises before he said it,' he recalled.

'I'd have given anything to see Hope's face,' Celia said longingly. 'Still, I expect she got the joke.'

'I think even she was a bit taken aback by that one. Toni said it would make her think carefully about what commands she gave him in future.'

'Does he always obey her commands?' Celia asked with interest.

'More or less. But don't think he's henpecked. Being devoted to her is what makes him happy.'

'Then he's the one who loves?'

'They love each other,' Francesco declared.

'No, I mean, that old saying about there's always one who loves and one who lets themselves be loved. He's the one who loves.'

'I suppose that's true,' Francesco said thoughtfully. 'I'd never realised it before, but I often see his eyes follow her around the room. With her it happens less.'

She didn't answer this, and when he stole a brief glance at her he saw that she was leaning back with her eyes closed, perhaps dozing.

At her apartment he opened the car door, handed her out, then did the same for Jacko, and watched as the dog took her to the front door.

'Can I come in for a moment?' he asked.

'Yes, of course.'

He forced himself to stay back as she allowed Jacko to take

her inside and knelt down to remove his harness. He immediately went to drink from his bowl, then flopped onto his bed.

'He looks a bit dispirited,' Francesco observed, 'not lively as Wicksy used to.'

'I know,' she said. 'I sense it. He works hard, but he's not happy.'

'You said he was with his last owner a long time?'

'That's true.'

'And then he got told to go?' Francesco mused.

'Well, not quite like that.'

'It probably felt like that to him. He doesn't understand the reasons. Everything he thought was secure was suddenly snatched away.'

'But the same thing happened to Wicksy, and he adjusted to his new owners,' Celia pointed out. 'When he was playing with those children he had that special note in his bark that means a dog's having the time of his life.'

'I suppose dogs have different personalities, like people. Wicksy got lucky, but it hasn't worked out so well with Jacko. How does he come to terms with his loss if nobody can explain it to him?'

Celia turned her head towards him, frowning at something she'd heard in his voice.

'What did you mean by that?' she asked.

'Nothing,' he said hastily. 'Nothing special.'

'Yes, you did. Tell me. Francesco, please, it's important. Tell me what you meant.'

'I'm not sure that I know. Just that it's something I seem to sense in my bones: being safe, and then not being safe and not understanding—'

'Tell me,' she said again, urgently.

'I can't. I don't know the words.'

Even as he spoke he felt the mood drain away from him, leaving him empty inside.

'I only meant—about Jacko,' he said heavily.

'Yes, of course.' Celia dropped to her knees and fondled Jacko, kissing and caressing his ears. 'Poor old boy,' she crooned. 'It's hard for you, isn't it?'

The animal responded by gazing up at her from gentle, yearning eyes. Francesco watched her hands moving over him, offering comfort, and suddenly he was back in another time.

The details were vague, but he recalled that he'd missed a contract he'd badly wanted and come home in a foul mood. She'd come up behind him as he'd sat glowering into a whisky, slipped her arms about him from behind, and dropped a kiss on top of his head.

'Don't let it get you down,' she'd murmured. 'It's not the end of the world.'

'Right now it feels like it,' he'd growled.

'Nonsense. Other things matter far more.'

'Like what?'

'Like this,' she'd said, proceeding to demonstrate.

In a few minutes they'd been in bed and the contract had been forgotten.

Now her caresses were wasted on a dog.

'Is Jacko looking any happier?' she asked.

'Yes, he only wanted you to show you love him. You can leave him now. He's all right.'

To his relief she did so, rising to her feet and turning in his direction. He reached out his hand and took hold of hers gently.

'You're beautiful,' he said. 'All evening I couldn't take my—my eyes off you.'

She smiled and moved closer to him. 'That's good,' she said. 'At one time you'd never have said that. You're learning fast.'

'You once said I'd never learn.'

'I underestimated you.'

'Sure, I'm a quick learner. If you bash me over the head a few times I get the point—even if it's too late.'

'Yes,' she echoed. 'That can be the worst of all. You look back and think—'

'If only,' he murmured.

'Yes—if only. If only I'd known then what I know now I'd have made better use of it. If only I was wiser and cleverer than I am—'

'I thought I was the one who wasn't wise or clever,' he said wryly.

'I wasn't so bright. I could have handled a lot of things better than I did.'

There was a melancholy in her voice that made his heart ache. So much between them. So much anger and misunderstanding, resentment, grief, yet so much warmth, so much joy and love. Where had it gone?

'Could you have done anything differently?' he asked. 'Could I? We are as we are. I think we were made to hurt each other—'

'And miss each other in the dark,' she said wistfully.

'But you're not afraid of the dark,' he reminded her.

Celia was standing very close to him, and it was natural to lay his hands on her bare shoulders, so that she turned her head up, almost as if she were looking at him, and spoke softly.

'No, but there are other things to be afraid of.'

'Not you,' he said at once. 'You were never afraid of anything.'

'I don't do so well with people, though, do I?' she whispered.

'Some people are beyond help,' he said heavily.

'Nobody is beyond help, if only—'

'Yes?' he murmured. 'If only—but it's a big "if only."'

'Francesco—'

She shook her head in a way that was almost helpless. It was so rare for her to be at a loss that it hurt him obscurely. His head seemed to lower itself without his will, until his cheek lay against hers.

He felt her tremble, but she didn't push him away, and he was emboldened to turn so that his lips brushed her face. She raised her hands and laid them on his shoulders, letting them drift inwards until they touched his neck. He drew back an inch so that he could look down into her face, trying to read her expression.

There was a gentleness in her face that he hadn't seen since she'd arrived in Naples, but more than that, a sort of wonder, as though she hadn't believed that this could still happen.

Francesco held his breath while she began to run her fingers over his face, tracing the shape of his jaw, his lean cheeks, the outline of his lips, making it hard for him to keep his rising feelings under control. If he'd dared yield to them he would have seized her up in his arms, kissed her until they were half out of their minds, then carried her to bed. It was what he'd done many times before. But now he forced himself to stay still, waiting to see if she would move so that her lips could meet his, and at last she did.

It was as though time had vanished. The kiss she gave him now was the kiss she had always given him, the one he wanted from her all his life.

He should be strong and resist it, but he had no strength where she was concerned.

Her lips teased his seductively, reminding him of things best forgotten. A man could lose his sanity with a woman like this. But while his mind worked his mouth was caressing hers in return, taking over the kiss, becoming the tender aggressor.

All was well again. They had never been apart, and never would be, because this was the only thing that mattered.

The shrill of the phone startled them. Francesco muttered a curse.

'I thought you turned it off.'

'That's the landline,' she said reluctantly. 'I'll have to answer it.'

She was shaking, but not as much as he was. Through her hands and her whole body she could sense the disturbance that racked him. She didn't want to answer the phone, but it would just ring until she did.

Francesco pulled away and snatched up the phone, barking, 'Hallo? No, she can't come to the phone right now…I don't care how urgent it is, you'll have to try later—'

'Who is it?' she asked.

'Sandro. Here!' He handed her the receiver. 'Get rid of him.'

His curt command acted like a burst of cold water cascading over her. He was trying to control her again.

'Sandro? I told you I'd call you back. Can't it wait?'

'No, we're about to lose our best chance of a really big customer,' came the voice down the phone, naming a man they'd been cultivating for days. 'He's about to leave town, but he wants to talk to you before he goes. Please, Celia, we really need this one.'

'Yes, we do,' she admitted. 'All right, I'll call him at once. I've got his number. Good night.' She hung up.

'So that's that?' Francesco said coldly. 'He says jump and you do.'

'I jump when the business needs me,' she said, equally coldly. 'Not Sandro.'

'To hell with business!'

'There's a thing I never thought to hear you say.'

'Couldn't you have put us first and work second?'

'I was going to,' she cried. 'Can't you understand that? I was going to put him off, but then you had to charge in like a steamroller, giving your orders, telling me what I could and couldn't do. Haven't you learned by now that I won't stand for that?'

'I'd better leave,' he snapped. 'You have a phone call to make.'

'You're right. Good night.'

As he departed she was already lifting the phone.

The conversation that followed was long, complex, and took all her skill to bring to a successful conclusion. She was left with a sense of triumph in her achievement, but also a sad awareness of the price she'd paid.

When she'd hung up the apartment seemed suddenly empty. It wasn't just the fact that she was alone. She was used to that. But there was a special quality to this aloneness, as though Francesco's anger was still imprinted on the air, still reproaching her with his absence.

It might have been so different, she thought despondently.

She undressed, settled Jacko down and got into bed, still aching with the yearning for what had nearly happened. She lay for a long time, wondering if nothing was truly all there would ever be.

A sound from the floor reminded her that she wasn't truly alone after all.

'Are you all right?' she asked Jacko, reaching down to touch him. 'You sound sad, poor old boy. Come up and join me, and we can be sad together.'

He nuzzled her hand, but otherwise didn't move.

'Come on,' she urged. 'Jump up on the bed with me. Never mind what they said at Guide Dog School about not getting on the furniture. I want you up here, where I can cuddle you.'

His mind relieved, he hopped onto the bed and snuggled against her. Celia buried her face against his warm fur.

'What would I do without you?' she murmured. 'You're the only real friend I have. You don't talk nonsense like him—or like me. You don't give me orders or try to control me and you understand everything without being told.'

His tongue flickered against her cheek and she smiled.

'Mmm! Do that again! That's nice. Thank you. You're beautiful. Everyone says so, and I know you are.'

They lay awhile in companionable silence while she stroked him.

'Shall I tell you a secret?' she asked after a while. 'I couldn't do it without my dogs. First Max, when I was a little girl, then Wicksy, now you. I go on a lot about my independence, but the truth is that it all depends on my furry friends. Don't tell on me, will you?'

He nudged her with his nose.

'Thanks. I knew I could rely on you. You see, without you I'd fall into the hands of a control freak like Francesco. I can only fight him by being as awkward as possible—and if there's one thing I do know about it's being awkward—but I can't do that without you there to prop up the illusion.'

She sighed despondently.

'Listen to me, talking about fighting him. I don't want to fight him. I want to love him. I call him a control freak, but he isn't really. It's just something that makes him act that way. I don't understand it, and I don't think he does. I still love him. I wish I didn't, but you can't just turn it off, can you?'

He gave a sad whine of agreement.

'Was I very stupid to come here?' she asked him. 'It seemed so easy when I planned it. If I could only meet him on his own ground we might start again and get it right this

ime. Now I wonder if that can ever happen. Tonight I even
1oped— It was going so well. I was remembering how much
love him, and why. When he kissed me it was just like
>efore, and I wanted him so much. Suddenly it seemed a
1undred years since we last made love, and I couldn't wait
'or it to happen again. All the things that came between us
lidn't matter any more, as long as I could belong to him and
<now that he belonged to me. Oh, Jacko, we were that close—
'hat close— If only—'

She sighed, forcing herself down to earth.

'But then Sandro phoned and it was like time had rolled
>ack. Francesco became the man I hate, taking control,
>arking orders. Everything has to be done his way, and I can't
>ear that. And then I was glad that the call came in time to stop
1s making love. Yes, I was. I was glad—really, really glad.'

Jacko pressed closer, giving her cheek a soft nudge of
;ympathy. He knew a lie when he heard one.

*

Francesco didn't contact Celia next day, but Olympia did.
She spent the afternoon being escorted around the factory,
naking verbal notes, and was then swept off to the apartment
vhere Olympia lived with her husband, Primo Rinucci.

As she was working on the evening meal and chatting to
Celia in the kitchen, the phone rang.

'*Ciao?*' she sang into the receiver. 'Yes, everything went
vell.' To Celia she said, 'It's Francesco. He wants to know
1ow your visit went.' She turned back to the receiver. 'We've
;ot lots of ideas to talk about.'

'Tell him to come over here,' Primo said from the doorway.
We'll mull the ideas over together.'

Then Olympia, talking into the phone, 'Come and join us for
iupper— Oh, nonsense! You can't have that much to do—'

Celia deciphered this without trouble. After last night Francesco didn't want to come where he would meet her. And he was right, she told herself firmly. Everything was falling apart again and he was wise to avoid her.

'Besides,' Olympia was saying, 'you introduced us to Celia, so you must come and hear how your protégée is doing. I'll lay another place. No argument. Get moving.'

She hung up.

'Does your brother ever stop working?' she complained to Primo.

'He took yesterday evening off for the party,' Celia said lightly. 'You can't expect him to rest for two evenings in a row. You know how driven he is about business.'

'Not really,' Primo said. 'He went abroad ten years ago, and stayed there until recently. None of us knows him really well.'

'Why did he go?' Celia asked.

'I'm not sure, but he was never at home much even before that. He travelled all over Italy, working a year here, a year there, always making money. He has the devil's touch about that. Then he'd get fed up and come back, only to leave again. At last he went to America, stayed there until three years ago, then went to England. I don't know why he wanders so much—what he's looking for. But maybe you can tell. You must know him better than anyone.'

'No,' Celia said, shaking her head. 'I don't really know him at all.'

Half an hour later there was a ring on the bell and Primo went to answer, returning with Francesco and Carlo.

'We met in the street,' Francesco announced.

'I just came to say hallo,' Carlo said, giving Celia a peck on the cheek.

'Stay for supper,' Olympia said.

'I can't. Della will be home soon,' Carlo explained, naming his wife, a television producer, who'd been forced to take a long rest owing to poor health.

'She's trying to take up the reins again,' he said, 'and she's gone to look at a place with a history that's given her an idea for a programme. She'll be expecting to find me at home.'

'Call her,' Primo said. 'Tell her to come here instead.'

While they argued about it Francesco sat beside Celia and said quietly, 'I gather things went well today?'

'Yes, I drummed up lots of business. There was a man there who'd come to sign a contract from another firm. He's booked me for an assessment visit, too, and he says he knows several other people who'd be interested. I'm going great guns.'

'I'm glad you're a success. Is Sandro pleased?'

'This has nothing to do with Sandro. Giving advice in the workplace is exclusively mine. Follia Per Sempre is another firm. I told you, Sandro and I don't do sensible.'

'Ah, yes, Sandro and you!' he said wryly.

'What does that mean?'

'It means what it sounds as though it means. It means that when he called last night you abandoned everything else. *Mio Dio,* you forgot me easily.'

'Some men are easy to forget.'

'Thank you.'

'And some are impossible to forget,' she murmured.

Silence. Hell would freeze over before he asked her into which category she had assigned him.

Now they could clearly hear Carlo talking to Della, explaining the change of plan.

'But only if you're not too tired,' he added quickly. 'You've been working hard all day, and now you've got the journey back—you should have let me come, too, and drive you

home—all right, all right—don't be mad at me. I know wha
we said, but—'

'You see, I'm not the only one,' Francesco said wryly t
Celia. 'He annoys Della as much as I annoy you.'

'Why?' she asked, refusing to rise to the bait. 'Is she re
ally as ill as all that?'

'She was in a plane crash, and had a heart attack immedi
ately afterwards. She'll always be frail, plus she's seven year
older than Carlo, and he's very protective of her.'

'Yes, I can hear. Poor Carlo, he sounds desperate. The sa
thing is that he's probably infuriating her and he doesn't knov
it.'

'Oh, he knows it all right,' Francesco said wryly. 'He jus
doesn't know how to stop.'

It became clear that this was true. Carlo wouldn't let it go
and the conversation ended so abruptly that Celia wondere
if Della had hung up. After that Carlo was on hot coals unti
she arrived half an hour later, full of eagerness and enthusiasm
for the day she had spent, and then he became happier.

CHAPTER SEVEN

OVER dinner the six of them plunged into a professional discussion in which everything was forgotten but the exchange of ideas. Celia came to vivid life, in command of her subject, thoroughly enjoying her expertise and the admiration that it won for her.

Carlo listened to her with particular interest. He was an archaeologist whose life had been spent on the move until he married. Then he'd taken a job running one of the Naples museums, enabling him to stay in one place for Della's sake.

It had been the sacrifice of a brilliant career, but he'd set himself to transform the museum, and had done it so well that he was becoming an authority in his new sphere.

'It's a pity there's so little scope for visual aids in a museum,' he mused. 'I'm not talking about employees, though. I'm putting some things in place to help them, and I'd be glad if you'd come and give me your opinion, Celia.'

'I'd love to. But if you're not talking about employees you must mean visitors?'

'That's right. How can I help them? They can listen to audio descriptions, but how much does that help? It doesn't tell you what a picture really looks like, or an ancient vase. I did try letting people run their hands over things, but the trustees went ballistic in case of breakages. Mind you, the only person who broke anything was the son of a trustee who had perfect eyesight—or would have done if he'd been sober at the time.'

Everybody laughed, but suddenly Francesco said, 'Why don't you make replicas?'

'They're no use,' Carlo said. 'I had a crowd of students in last week all trying to copy a Greek statue. Some of the results were good, but they couldn't have passed for the original.'

'I don't mean that,' Francesco said. 'There's some computer software that'll take a thousand photos from every angle. You can use these to make a three-dimensional virtual model, which the computer then turns into a real model by giving instructions to another machine. The result is an exact likeness, except that it's made of resin. Every little scratch and dent is duplicated. If it's a statue, you can even see the chisel marks. People can pick it up to study it. If it gets damaged, no problem. You just tell the computer to make another. You could copy every artifact in the place and make them available to everyone—not just the people who can't see.'

'That's right,' Celia said. 'Why should we have all the privileges? Francesco, it's a marvellous idea.'

'Yes, it is,' Carlo agreed. 'You're a dark horse, brother.'

'He hides his light under a bushel,' Celia said, smiling.

She was suddenly very happy, as though Francesco had reached out to her in a new way. And the next moment she felt his hand seeking hers under the table.

She hadn't been wrong about him, she thought joyfully. Everything was still possible.

As they were all leaving to go she said to him, 'I hope you're going to offer me a lift home.'

'Of course. I'll fetch your jacket.'

On the way he passed Carlo and Della, who had resumed their argument.

'Be careful,' he said, laying his hand on his brother's shoulder. 'The belief that you're doing the right thing can be the biggest trap there is, and the most destructive.'

'Did you fall into it?' Della asked.

'Big-time. Celia and I—well—'

Briefly he explained the circumstances of their parting.

'I thought I was taking care of her,' he finished, 'but I was simply making her want to bang her head against the wall.'

He saw the other two give each other a quick glance, then Carlo's arm went around his wife's shoulders and he dropped a kiss onto her head.

'Just don't let it happen to you two, that's all,' Francesco said. 'Good night.'

When he'd gone Della looked up at her husband, holding him tightly.

'I don't know why you said Francesco was a hard man,' she said. 'I think he's lovely, kind and sensitive. I hadn't expected him to have such insight.'

'Me, neither,' Carlo said. 'I'm beginning to wonder if any of us have ever understood the first thing about him.'

As he drove home to Celia's apartment Francesco said, 'How's this for a plan? I'll collect you tomorrow and we'll go to my factory so that you can give it the once-over and tell me what needs doing.'

'That sounds lovely, but I'm booked tomorrow,' she said regretfully.

'Sure—I was forgetting that your diary's getting crowded. What is it? A rival factory?'

'No, I'm working with Sandro. We're investigating new activities to offer people.'

'Mad activities?' he asked lightly.

'The madder the better.'

'I'll be there to give you a lift.'

'Without even asking me where we're going and why?'

'Does it matter?'

'It might be something you disapprove of.'

'I have no right to disapprove,' he said expansively. 'You are your own mistress, and you make your own decisions.' He was full of goodwill towards the world, and for once it was easy to say the right thing.

'Excuse me? Can I have that in writing?' she asked sceptically.

'It's none of my business,' he declared, warming to his theme and enjoying her astonishment. 'I have no opinions, and if I had I wouldn't dream of inflicting them on you.'

'You're an impostor,' she said firmly. 'Where have you hidden the real Francesco Rinucci? He would never have said anything like that.'

'I'm a reformed character. Now, what time shall I collect you tomorrow?'

She gave him the time, and he dropped her outside the apartment building. His last view was of her following Jacko inside. He drove away, remembering the previous night and wondering how things could have changed so quickly for the better.

Francesco was there on time the next afternoon, smiling with pleasure at the sight of her, beautiful in white linen pants and blue shirt. But his smile faded as they were driving away and she gave him their destination.

'That's an airfield,' he said.

'That's right. A small, private airfield about five miles outside Naples.'

'To do what?' he asked ominously.

'Skydiving. It's all the rage among people who want a new experience.'

'Skydiving? You're going to do a parachute jump?' he demanded, so appalled that he had to swerve to avoid an accident.

'No, just Sandro. He's jumping out of a plane, but I have to be there to talk to the people on the ground—negotiations, sponsorship, etcetera.'

'The two of you are as insane as each other.'

'Well, we told you that,' she said patiently. 'It's the whole point. Anyway, like you said, you have no opinions one way or the other.'

'I never said anything as daft as that.'

'Yes, you did. You also said it was none of your business.'

After a moment he managed to say, 'On second thoughts, I can bear, with fortitude, the sight of Sandro risking his neck.'

She chuckled, understanding perfectly.

'Never mind about Sandro,' she said.

'I don't. I don't think about him from one hour to the next.' Then he added thoughtlessly, 'Mind you, I might wish he were less good-looking.'

'*Is* he good-looking?' she demanded with suspicious eagerness. 'Oh, do tell me, because I've always wondered. Is he really, *really* handsome?'

Francesco ground his teeth. 'I walked right into that, didn't I?' he asked.

'Well, you were a little incautious,' she teased. 'Go on, tell me.'

'No way. You know exactly what he looks like, because you got someone to tell you with the first meeting.'

'You don't know that.'

'Yes, I do, because it's what you did with me.'

There was a slight pause before she said, 'What I did with you, and what I do with other people—well, they're not the same thing at all.'

'Are you going to tell me what that means?' he asked cautiously.

'With you, it mattered. Is it far to this place?'

'Not long now,' he said, accepting her change of subject. He needed time to think. Things were moving with dizzying speed.

After an hour's drive they reached the little airfield, already busy with several private planes. At the offices they were met by a small crowd. Amid the introductions Francesco gained an impression of a local journalist, a businessman considering becoming a backer and several charities who stood to gain from sponsorship.

'Did you fix all this?' Francesco asked.

'Of course. This is my side of things.'

'I'm impressed. But I always knew you were efficient.'

He concealed his relief that she had no thoughts of flying, and even allowed himself a moment of complacency at his own tact.

The pilot appeared with Sandro, already dressed up and strapped into his parachute. Behind him came another man, similarly dressed. This was Sandro's skydiving partner.

'We take off,' Sandro said, 'climb to about thirteen thousand feet and circle the airport twice before jumping.'

'How far do you fall before opening the parachute?' Celia wanted to know.

'Down to about two and a half thousand feet,' Sandro replied.

'As low as that?' Francesco queried in surprise.

'Well, the whole point is to freefall as far as possible,' the pilot said. 'The parachute is just to break the fall at the last minute.'

'Otherwise you'd be killed,' Sandro observed cheerfully.

'Which would seriously spoil your enjoyment of the next jump,' Celia supplied, and they punched the air together.

The journalists thoroughly enjoyed this exchange, Francesco noted sourly.

'Will you look after my dog for me?' Sandro asked Celia.

'Sure.' She took the harness, but then found herself rather encumbered with two animals and her bag.

'Give Jacko to me,' Francesco said.

'Good idea. You and he seem to be on each other's wave-length.'

'Now you're just being fanciful,' he said, half fondly, half in exasperation.

'No, I'm not. He heard what you said about having his security snatched away, and he knows you understand him.'

Outwardly he dismissed her words. And yet it seemed to him that Jacko moved towards him willingly and sat close to his leg, as though contented.

I'm getting over-imaginative, he thought.

'What's happening now?' Celia asked.

'They're walking away towards the aircraft. It's just a tiny one, barely enough for the three of them—nearly there—someone's taking a last look at the parachutes—the pilot's climbing aboard and reaching back to help Sandro.'

Then he heard something that froze his blood. It was the softest possible sound, but it raised ghastly spectres, howling death and despair at him.

It was a sigh of envy.

He gave a sharp glance at Celia, hoping he'd imagined it, but there was no mistaking the way her head was thrown back, as though she could see up into the sky, or the look of ecstasy on her face.

Envy. Delight. Determination. All the things that would make a rational man bang his head against the nearest brick wall. And when he'd done that he would shoot himself, or jump off a cliff, whichever seemed most likely to promote health, happiness and sanity.

What he would *not* do was involve himself with this woman a second time. He would never again put it in her power to break his heart with her outrageous, wilful, insane, dotty-headed enthusiasms. That was out, finished, done with.

'Are you all right?' Celia asked, reaching for him in alarm.

'Of course I am,' he snapped. 'Why?'

'You're trembling.'

'No, just a bit chilly.'

'It's windy. They should have a good flight. What are they doing now?'

'They've just closed the plane door—now they're starting to move—gathering speed.'

'I can hear the engine. They've left the ground, haven't they?'

'Yes, the plane is climbing—climbing—almost out of sight—'

'But it's coming back soon?' she asked anxiously, almost like a child fearful of being denied a treat.

'It's coming back now, circling the airfield—it's almost out of sight—lucky it's a clear day—I can just make it out…'

His voice trailed off. When she could bear the silence no longer Celia squealed, *'Well?'*

'I think Sandro and his partner are jumping now—yes, there they go!'

Way above him in the blue he could just make out the two men, leaving the aircraft together and going into freefall.

'What are they doing?' she cried, in the anguish of unbear-able tension. 'Have they opened their parachutes yet?'

'No, they're still holding on to each other—coming lower—lower—I can see them clearly now—they're going to have to open up any minute—aren't they?'

The hair-raising possibility of a last-minute disaster was there in his voice, and in the gasps from the crowd that turned to cheers as the men released each other and two parachutes opened, letting them glide gracefully earthwards.

'They've landed,' Francesco said. 'They're both safe.'

'Wonderful!' Celia rejoiced. 'Now we've really got some-thing spectacular to offer.'

Francesco pulled himself together. There would be time for his misgivings later. Just now he would concentrate on saying and doing the right things to get the business over with quickly. So he assumed a bright smile and prepared to say something suitable. But before he could do so Celia was sur-rounded by journalists, all hurling questions at her. She replied eagerly, leaving Francesco and Jacko to retire discreetly into the background.

'That's put us in our place,' he commiserated with the dog. 'We're definitely not needed just now.' He scratched the silky head. 'I guess we both know how that feels.'

A soft grunt was his answer.

'I wonder what your folks were like,' he mused. 'I guess you loved them, and then they said, "Get out!" And that was that. You're coping somehow but—'

He stopped himself in alarm.

'Listen to me, talking to you as if you understood. But maybe you do. She thinks so. I expect she talks to you, doesn't she? She used to talk to Wicksy a lot. I wonder what she says about me.'

But he was only trying to distract his own attention from what had happened inside his head. As often before, the words, *Get out!* had acted like a malign spell, causing the universe to spin with terrifying speed before settling down into a bleak place.

'What the devil's the matter with me?' he muttered. 'Why does it happen? *Why?*'

They weren't the only words Celia had hurled at him, nor the cruelest. So why? He asked himself that again and again, but there was no answer. If he could have discovered one, he felt he might have begun to find his way out of the maze.

'Francesco?' It was Celia's voice, calling him back from a trance, and her hand shaking his shoulder. 'Are you all right?'

'Yes, of course. Where shall I take you now? Are you having dinner with your new contacts? With Sandro?'

'No, we've set up meetings for next week. Let's go home.'

There was a shout. Sandro was approaching, hailing them.

'What a day! So many new opportunities. Not just jumping from planes, but from balloons.'

'That'll really be something to try!' Celia exclaimed. 'Just wait until we get talking next week.'

'Fine, I'll see you then,' Sandro said, using the word *see* in the casual fashion that always startled Francesco. 'Goodbye, *cara.*'

He put an arm around Celia's shoulder, drew her close and gave her a hearty kiss. She kissed him back. To Francesco it seemed an age before they could get away, and even then she had to dash back to Sandro to say something she'd forgotten. But at last they were in the car on the way home.

'Let's do some shopping and I'll cook you supper.'

The next hour was pure pleasure. This was how they'd been at their happiest—planning meals, shopping together. She would let him choose the vegetables, and sometimes the meat, although she really preferred her own judgement for meat.

'You were always a good cook,' he recalled as they worked out the menu, walking around the grocer's. 'You made a list of all my favourite dishes and practised until you could do them perfectly.'

'But some of the Italian ones I'd never heard of,' she remembered.

'And you wanted me to show you how to make them. As though I knew a potato from a bean! My expertise stopped at eating them.' He laughed suddenly. 'Do you remember how shocked you were?'

'Yes, I thought all Italian men were great cooks.'

'I'm part English,' he reminded her defensively. 'That's the part of me that's useless. And you actually went out and took a course in Italian cookery—'

'What is it?' she asked, for he had fallen silent abruptly.

'Nothing. I just suddenly remembered how determined you are. That cooking school said you were their best pupil.'

'When I want something I stop at nothing,' she said lightly. 'Ruthless and unprincipled, that's me.'

'I guess. Only it didn't feel like ruthless and unprincipled. It felt like being spoiled rotten. I loved it.'

'So did I,' she said softly.

'Only…' he hesitated, then said, 'Only I wanted to look after you, too.'

'I know.'

'I can't just sit there with my feet up, being waited on by the little woman.'

'Not unless you want the little woman to thump you over the head with a saucepan,' she chuckled.

'As you say. Sometimes I wanted you to put *your* feet up.'

'Only sometimes?'

'Just sometimes,' he said hastily. 'I'm enough of a chauvinist porker for that.'

This time they laughed together, and reached the checkout in perfect accord.

The goodwill lasted as they returned to her home and unpacked in her kitchen. In an ecstasy of helpfulness he volunteered to take Jacko out for the necessary walk.

'Don't worry,' he assured his canine friend. 'I used to do this for Wicksy. I know the drill.'

Celia was just getting ready to serve the first course when her menfolk returned.

'The first course is cold,' she said, 'So that's all right, but I wanted to wait until you were here before I put the light under the pans.'

'Why? Is there something you want me to do?' he asked, missing the note in her voice that would have warned him she was about to make some outrageous joke.

'Just keep an eye on the lighted gas,' she informed him solemnly. 'Because—' she moved closer and lowered her voice melodramatically '—I can't see. I thought you knew that.'

For a moment her innocent manner almost fooled him, then he gave a gasp of shock.

'Celia, you little wretch!' he exploded. 'When will you stop doing that?'

'Never,' she cried, rejoicing as his hands clasped her shoulders and gave them a little shake. 'If anyone else said it, it would be vulgar and insensitive, but I can say what I like. Oh, darling, your face!'

'You don't know what my face looks like.'

'Oh, yes, I do,' she crowed. 'I know exactly what it looks like. You're thinking, How can she *say* a thing like that?'

'That's putting it very mildly. Oh, *you*—'

His grip tightened, pulling her against him, and the next moment she felt what she had been scheming for the last few minutes—his mouth on hers, urgent and frustrated, just as she wanted it. His whole body was shaking with the desire he'd been controlling, and she rejoiced in the sensation of having him in her hands, in her arms, almost under her control.

'You,' he muttered, between raining fierce kisses on her face. 'You—you—'

'What about me?' she asked, kissing and laughing together.

'Just that you're— Come here!'

This time there was no way she could talk against the caressing pressure of his mouth. For too long she'd lived without the fulfilment that only he could give her, and now her body clamoured for him as achingly as her heart had done for months.

Two nights ago they had come so close to finding each other again, but Sandro's call had interrupted them. Now nothing would get in the way. Just before leaving the airfield she'd warned Sandro not to call her tonight, just as she'd previously warned—or perhaps promised—Francesco, she was ruthless and unprincipled in getting what she wanted.

He was hers, and the time had come to make that clear. Her determination infused every movement of her swift fingers, finding buttons to undo, pulling his shirt out of his trousers, caressing his skin, inciting him with every skilful movement at her command while keeping her mouth against his and her tongue teasing him wickedly.

'Celia,' he gasped, 'do you know what you're doing?'

'I do— Do you?' she managed to gasp.

'It's too late to change your mind.'

'*Who's changing her mind?*'

That was it. Now nothing could have stopped him. Scooping her up with more vigour than gallantry, he strode into her room and collapsed onto the bed with her in his arms. Undressing each other was difficult while they were so intricately entangled, but they managed somehow, working through the layers, getting in each other's way, laughing exultantly, getting it wrong, getting it right, trying to control the mounting pleasure long enough to reach their goal, and finally reaching it with long sighs of satisfaction.

'Oh, yes,' she murmured, half out of her mind with what she had wanted for so long and so hopelessly.

The feel of having him inside her again was so good that she wondered how she'd survived so long without it. She moved strongly against him, seeking to repeat the first, unrepeatable sensation. She wanted to touch him all over at the same time—his arms, his neck, his wide shoulders and muscular torso. Then she wanted to slide her hands down the length of him to the narrow hips and long muscular thighs. In their frenzy of action all she could manage was to wrap her own thighs around him, enclosing him, drawing him deep into her body as she wanted him deep in her heart.

They climaxed together almost at once, and continued without a pause, their desire barely touched, far from slaked. Other lovings had taught them that they could inspire each other for a long time before they were satisfied. But there had never been a loving like this.

As he lay over her afterwards, looking down into her face, Celia had one of her rare moments of wishing for sight. She longed to see his face and find in it the tenderness she'd felt in his touch. But then he kissed her gently, and she knew that she had all she needed. He moved off her while still holding her in his arms, so that she was pulled over against him, heart to heart.

'Are you all right?' he asked softly, as he had always done before.

Her answer was the same as then, a little sound of blissful content, for there were some emotions that no words could express. He responded by holding her closer and burying his face in her hair.

'I was afraid I'd lost you for good,' he said.

'You couldn't lose me,' she murmured against his skin.

She went on whispering incoherent words, wondering how it was possible to be so happy.

Somewhere above her head he gave a brief laugh.

'What is it?' she asked at once.

'I was remembering our first night together. I'd been trying to imagine what you wore underneath, and I'd decided it must be something practical, because you were so fiercely efficient.'

'But it wasn't practical at all, was it?'

'No way. A satin thong that practically didn't exist, and a satin and lace bra, all in brilliant scarlet.'

'Did you disapprove?'

'No, I loved it. I knew then that I'd underestimated you.'

'You always did.'

'And you're wearing them again today.'

'You mean, I *was* wearing them, don't you?' she teased.

'Yes, I guess I do.'

She smiled to herself. She'd never told him that she'd bought the sexy underwear after their first evening together, when she'd spent that lonely week, longing for him to return, determined to be ready for anything if he did. And when she'd set out for Naples, determined to reclaim him, it was the first thing she'd packed.

For the moment she'd triumphed. Whatever their problems were they had faded to nothing. Perhaps she would remember them one day. Or perhaps not. It hardly seemed to matter.

CHAPTER EIGHT

'DO YOU know what we need now?' Francesco asked sleepily.

'What?'

'Champagne. I don't suppose you keep any?'

'I might just have some,' she said, carefully casual.

In fact, she'd laid in a store of that, too, but there was no need for him to know that.

They rose from the bed and stood for a moment leaning against each other, like two people who'd come to the end of a long and exhausting race and needed time to recover before enjoying the prize.

Afterwards she donned a satin robe, while he pulled on his trousers and followed her into the kitchen where she produced the champagne and two glasses. He poured them both a glass, and they clinked.

'I've just discovered I'm tired,' he said.

'That's a pity, because I've got plans for you later.'

'Have mercy, woman.'

'Slacker,' she jeered.

'Not at all. But let's stretch out on the sofa first.'

They did so, with her sitting and him lying with his head on her leg.

'I could stay like this for ever,' he said blissfully.

'Me, too.'

'It's how we used to be.'

'And now we've got it back,' she murmured. 'How could we have been so careless?'

'We never will be again. In future we'll—' he made a vague gesture '—discuss things rationally.'

She chuckled. 'Shall I give you lessons in that?'

'Oi, cheeky!'

'Rationally!' she mocked. 'You wouldn't recognise rational discussion if it bopped you on the nose.'

'OK, you may have to give me a few lessons, but we'll get there. I'm not going to lose you a second time just because— *Oh, hell!*'

The last remark was jerked from him by the ringing of the telephone.

'If that's Sandro, just let me speak to him for five seconds,' Francesco begged.

'It won't be, I promise.' Celia reached for the phone, which was on a small table at the end of the sofa. 'Hallo? *Ciao,* Mario.'

Suddenly she sounded pleased, and Francesco's head rose from her leg in query.

'Journalist,' she mouthed. 'He was there this afternoon.'

'Then he should have talked to you this afternoon.'

'He did. Mario, it's not a good time…oh, I see…when's your deadline? All right, just five minutes, as long as you promise me a great story. And Sandro, of course…he had a great time, so he told me afterwards…oh, yes, green with envy…my turn soon. But I may jump from a helicopter, or a balloon. That way we cover the whole range…yes, you can say that. And there's one other thing—'

After a few moments she hung up, aware that something had

changed. It wasn't just that Francesco's head had vanished from her leg. The atmosphere was suddenly spiky and dangerous.

'What is it?' she asked, feeling for him.

'You just said that to make a good story, right? About jumping? You're not going to do that.'

After a brief silence she said, 'Are you asking me or telling me?' Her voice was quiet, but suddenly it had an edge.

'*Cara*, please! Let's not go into this again. We said it would be different this time. You've had your fun. You've turned me white haired with fear often enough—'

'Had my fun?' she echoed, aghast. 'Is that how you see it?'

'I've heard you call it fun.'

'Among other things. Sure, it's fun, but that's not why I live as I do. It's because I won't be pigeonholed as "disabled"— by you or anyone else.'

'All right,' he said, making a belated attempt to stop the world disintegrating a second time. 'But you've done those things, and I've put up with—*accepted* it. Surely it's time to—that is, we've talked and I thought you understood—'

'You mean, you thought I'd given in,' she said slowly.

'I thought you'd seen reason— No, I didn't mean that—'

'Why not? It's honest. I don't mind you saying things like that. What I mind is your assumption that if I dare to disagree with you I'm off my head. Well, I do disagree, and it's time *you* saw reason.'

With disaster looming on the road ahead Francesco tried— he really tried—to avoid it. But stark terror was taking him over again, as so often in the past, making him forget everything he'd learned.

'It *isn't* reasonable for you to carry on like this,' he snapped. 'One day you'll get killed. Am I supposed to just shrug and say, "Oh, well, it doesn't matter?" If I protest it's because I love you.'

'But with you love becomes control,' Celia cried. 'It's not just dangerous things, it's everything. You never felt that I had the right to my own life.

I won't be treated as someone who can't do what other people take for granted. Above all I won't have you telling me what I can and can't do. Oh, God, why are we talking like this—*again?*'

Her voice rose to a shriek as the truth hit her. It struck him, too, in the same moment. Aghast, they regarded the ruin that had come upon them so suddenly.

'Look,' he said at last, 'let's forget this. We don't know what we're saying. Before the phone rang—'

'We were living in a fool's paradise,' she exclaimed in despair. 'But it couldn't have lasted. This was always going to happen.'

'I won't admit that loving each other is a fool's paradise,' he said stubbornly.

She gave a bleak little laugh. 'It could be—for some people. Shouldn't we just admit it?'

'That's a terrible thing to say. It's like saying there's no such thing as love.'

'Perhaps it's just one of those things I can't do the way other people do,' she said bitterly. 'Maybe you were right about that, and it's time I listened. Diving in water or out of planes—fine! But a normal human relationship is beyond me—because it has to be on the terms I lay down, and they're too harsh for other people. Or maybe just too selfish. After all, what have I said? That you've got to let me do what I want all the time? Even I can hear the selfishness in that, but anything else suffocates me.'

'Don't talk like that,' he said violently. 'You're not selfish. It's just that I— Oh, let's just forget it.'

'How can we when it's always there?'

She turned away to hide the fact that she was beginning to cry, and he immediately reached out, trying to hold on to her.

'*Cara,* please—'

'Let me go.'

She pulled herself out of his grasp and turned away, not heeding where she was going. The next moment she'd collided with the doorjamb and reeled back.

'Celia—'

'No, no. I'm all right.'

'You're not all right. Your lip's bleeding. Come here.'

She seemed ready to fight him, but then she gave up and let him lead her to the sofa and make her sit down.

'It's nothing,' she said. 'I often bump into things.'

He shook his head. 'No, you don't,' he said in despair. 'I've never seen it happen before. It was my fault. I'm so sorry—'

'It wasn't your fault. You didn't push me. It was an accident. Francesco, please, *please*—why must you take every little thing to heart?'

'I don't know. It's just that—' He shook his head, as though by this means he could clear his confusion. 'I've always been that way, but suddenly I became worse, and it's grown out of control and made a monster of me.'

'You're not a monster,' she hastened to say.

'No, just a man it suffocates you to live with. And perhaps even I am beginning to see why. I guess I've turned into a bully again, haven't I?'

'Francesco, please, I never said you were a bully—'

'Not tonight. But the last time—when we broke up.'

'You remember that?'

'I remember every word. I'm even glad now that you said it.'

'It was cruel and untrue—'

'No, it was cruel and true. Which means it wasn't cruel at all. It needed saying. You'd been thinking it for a long time and biting it back—'

'No—'

'Celia, *carissima,* you've always been honest to the point of brutality, and I mean that as compliment. Don't weaken now. That night—when we came home after your dive and we quarrelled—you didn't say *bully* like someone who'd just thought of it. You said it like someone who'd been suppressing it for ages. If there's anything to regret, it's that you didn't say it before. We might have—'

He broke off. The thought was too painful to put into words.

'Yes,' she said huskily. 'We might have managed better. Who knows?'

In the silence he reached out his hand and touched her hair very gently. She turned her head at once, so that her cheek brushed his palm, and for a moment they stayed like that, aching with memory.

He was almost sure that he felt a touch of moisture on his hand, but he didn't ask if she were crying. He was afraid of breaking the spell.

'Celia…' was as much as he dared to say, in a voice no louder than a murmur.

She raised her head so that she was facing him, and he couldn't believe that she was blind. It was all there in her eyes—everything they'd had, everything they'd lost. And he knew that it must be in his own eyes, as well. She couldn't see it, but surely she would know? Because she knew everything

He longed to comfort her, to promise that he'd make everything all right for her. But how could he when what was wrong was himself?

He'd dreamed of finding a miracle, but now, reluctantly

he had to recognise that there were no miracles. The time had come to free her for the better life she would find without him.

'*Carissima*,' he said softly, 'let us talk.'

'Not yet,' she said in a muffled voice. 'Please, not yet.'

So she knew. Of course she did. Perhaps she'd come to Naples for him, hoping that they might have a second chance. She'd never told him that, but a thousand things had made him hope. Now he knew hope was futile, and so did she.

'Not yet,' she repeated.

'No,' he murmured. 'Not yet. We can have a little more time.'

A little time to hope for the miracle that would never happen. A little time before the pain would have to be faced. Finally.

He went into the bathroom and came out with a damp flannel to clean the graze on her lip. A tiny bruise was just beginning. Now it didn't seem right that they were almost naked.

'I'll get dressed,' he said.

But then he dropped his head and lay his lips against her breast. She drew a shuddering breath and tried to clasp her hands about his head, but he rose quickly and left her. After a moment she, too, moved into the bedroom to get dressed.

'Perhaps I should go now,' he said heavily.

Before she could reply the doorbell shrilled.

'I'm not expecting anyone,' she said. 'Would you go?'

Outside her front door he found a man in his fifties with an eager, nervous look.

'Does Signorina Ryland live here?' he asked. 'I was told she did.'

At the sound of his voice something happened to Jacko. He'd been curled up peacefully, but suddenly his head lifted and he was alert with his whole body. A soft 'Wuff!' escaped him.

Francesco ushered him in. Celia emerged to face the new-comer, frowning slightly.

'*Signorina,*' the man said earnestly, 'I am Antonio Feltona, and I have come to beg you to grant me a favour.'

'Feltona,' she murmured, then her brow cleared. 'Jacko was yours, wasn't he?'

'That's true. Then my sight came back and I no longer needed a guide dog.'

'And they gave him to me because I need someone with his experience in this city,' she recalled. 'Have you come to make sure he's all right? Here he is.'

As she spoke Jacko leapt up, yelping with delight, and hurled himself on his old master. Antonio dropped to his knees and embraced the eager dog, cooing affection into his ears.

'That's what's been wrong with Jacko all this time,' Francesco murmured.

'Something has been wrong?' the man asked.

'Only that he's seemed a bit listless, and not very happy,' Francesco explained.

'Yes,' Signor Feltona said, rising. 'My family loves him, and he loves us. When I regained my sight it seemed natural for him to be given to someone who needed him, but I think he was too old to make this move. And so I have come to ask you—to plead with you—to let us have him back.'

'What?' Celia was thunderstruck.

'I know it will be hard for you, but there are other dogs.'

'Not for me,' she said, agitated. 'It's his years of experience that make him valuable to me in the way a young dog couldn't be. No, I'm sorry. I can't do without him.'

'Please, *signorina,* won't you even think about it for a while?'

'No, there's nothing to think about. I'm sorry. It's out of the question.'

Celia turned and fled towards the kitchen door, her hands outstretched to prevent another collision. She just managed to avoid the wall, but it was a near thing.

It distressed her that Francesco should have seen this happen. After all she'd said about independence. How he would gloat!

But then his hands were on her gently, his voice in her ear.

'Steady, *carissima*. Just a little to your left. Just here.'

He edged her through the door into the kitchen and towards a chair.

'Sit down and I'll pour you a drink.'

She sat, trying to understand what was happening to her. She'd always been proud of her own confident efficiency, but suddenly she was swamped by fear. It swept over her in waves, making coherent thought impossible. Instead of giving calm consideration to the proposal, she'd blurted out her terrified resistance.

She felt a glass pushed into her hand and drank it without asking what it was. It was brandy.

'Thanks. I needed that,' she said huskily. 'Poor man. I didn't mean to shout at him.'

'It's not like you to lose it,' he said gently.

'I don't know what came over me. It's just that—I rely on Jacko so much. He's my lifeline. Another dog wouldn't be the same.'

'He could be trained to be as good. After a while it would be exactly the same.'

'But that would take time. This place is still new to me— Oh, I know I'm being selfish. You're right about Jacko. He's done his duty faithfully, but I've always sensed something not quite right, and now I know what it is. His heart's breaking. I ought to let him go, but how can I? I'd be lost without him.'

It passed across Fransesco's mind that she hadn't been los|
without *him*, but he banished the jealous thought quickly
overtaken by another thought, one so startling that he pulle|
away from her to walk the room lest his eagerness show too
clearly in his manner.

It was impossible, and yet…

'He's not the only dog in the world,' he began carefully
'You'd have had to have another one eventually.'

'But if he goes now, what can I do?'

He drew a slow breath. Now was his last chance to draw back
from the colossal risk he was about to take. But there would be
no drawing back. It was the biggest gamble of his life, but he
must take it or lose her. And she was worth everything.

'You can use me,' he said.

She turned her head sharply, as if staring at him.

'What did you say?'

'Let me be your dog. Make use of me.'

'Francesco, be serious.'

'I am serious,' he said, walking back and dropping down
on his knees beside her. 'Listen to me, Celia. I know I sound
crazy, but you're the one who's always talking about the
virtues of craziness.'

'For me, not for you,' she protested.

'You think I'm not good enough to be crazy, huh? Let
me show you.'

'*Caro*, this is madness. You don't know what you're sug|
gesting. You'd have to be with me constantly. What about
your own work?'

'That can manage without me for a while. What is it, Celia
Can't you trust me? I can do the job as well as a dog, I swear
it. I know all the commands—stop, start, stand, sit. I'll even
wear a harness.'

His clowning made her laugh, but there was still a serious doubt in her heart.

'I know you mean it,' she said, 'and it's a wonderful offer. But it would be so much harder than you think.'

'I'll do everything your way. When you don't need me, you won't even know I'm there. Isn't that enough?'

She hesitated, not knowing how to put it into words, and at last he came to her rescue.

'Once a bully, always a bully,' he said softly.

'No—*no*—'

'The dog is your independence, but that means independence from me. I should have understood that.'

'I don't always want to be independent from you,' she said in despair.

'I know, but we can't—*I* can't seem to stop blurring the lines. Knowing when to back off is something I never learned. I could try but—well, you know me. The man who shuts his ears.'

'Don't—please don't,' she whispered.

'I'm not saying that to be unkind, just reminding you that you got it right about me. You made your decision for us to part and it was a good one.'

'A good one for you?' she whispered.

He sighed and leaned his forehead against hers.

'It'll never be good for me without you. But I'm not good for you. It took me too long to see that, and if I'd had any sense I'd never have suggested taking Jacko's place. You keep him as long as you need him. Trusty friends are hard to replace.'

'Yes, I'd better go back and tell them.' She reached for his arm. 'It's all right,' she said. 'I can find my way, but I'm clinging to you for moral support.'

'I do have some uses,' he said lightly. 'Let's go.'

He stopped, silenced by the sight that met him as they entered the other room. Signor Feltona was sitting on the sofa with Jacko at his feet. The dog's head was turned up to him in an attitude of adoration.

'What is it?' she asked in a hurried under-voice.

'It's them—the way they're sitting together.'

Signor Feltona heard them and looked up quickly, his face full of hope that died when he saw their faces.

'Please—' he said.

'I can't—just yet,' Celia told him. 'But I'll get in touch with the society and ask for another dog very quickly. So you might get him back soon. That really is the best I do.'

The man's shoulders sagged, and so did Jacko's, it seemed to Francesco. He told himself to stop being sentimental, but there was an air of misery about the dog that suggested he'd followed what was happening.

'I see,' Signor Feltona said heavily. 'I had hoped—my children love him so much—but I may tell them that they can still hope?'

'I'll do it as soon as I can,' Celia assured him. 'I'm sorry. It's just—'

'I understand,' he said in a husky voice. 'I'll leave you now.'

He rose and prepared to be gone. A soft whine broke from Jacko.

'It's all right, boy,' he said. 'Stay. Maybe later. Now, say goodbye to me.'

He dropped to one knee and embraced Jacko, who whined again in misery.

'All right, now. We'll be together again soon, I promise. No, no—you mustn't do that. Get down, boy.'

'What is it?' Celia asked.

'He's trying to go, too,' Francesco said.

'It's nothing,' Signor Feltona said hurriedly. 'He's just a little distressed. Please don't be angry with him. He's a good boy.'

'Of course he is,' Celia said. 'Come here, Jacko.'

She held out her hand. For a moment it seemed that Jacko would defy her, but then he seemed to abandon hope and moved slowly forward until he was in front of her.

'Goodbye,' said Signor Feltona, turning towards the door.

Jacko didn't move, but a wail of such anguish broke from him that it froze everyone who heard it. He laid his snout in Celia's hand while wave upon wave of despair came from his throat as a lifetime's discipline struggled with heartbreak.

'Wait!' Celia called. 'Don't go. Francesco, stop him.'

'No need,' Francesco said, going to where their visitor was standing frozen, joy and disbelief warring on his face. 'Come back, *signore.*'

'Go on,' Celia said, giving Jacko a little push.

Nothing would have stopped him then. The dog bounded across the room to hurl himself into his old owner's arms so fiercely that the two of them landed on the sofa.

'Forgive me,' Antonio said, recovering some poise but still clinging to Jacko. 'Do you mean—'

'Jacko belongs with you,' Celia said. 'He can't bear to be parted from you. I won't force him to stay.'

'You mean it?' he asked incredulously. 'You really mean it?'

'I mean every word. Take him with you now, and I'll make it all right with the society.'

'But what will you do before you get a new dog?' Having got what he wanted, Antonio was suddenly assailed by conscience.

'Don't worry about me,' Celia said. 'I have a friend who will look after me. Now, take Jacko quickly.'

'First we say thank you,' Feltona said. He touched Jacko gently, whispering, 'Go.'

She dropped to her knees for one last embrace and the dog came into her arms—willingly this time. Francesco watched as he nuzzled her and she buried her face against him. When she released him he put up a paw as if to have one last contact.

He understands, Francesco thought. He's a dog, but he knows she's made a sacrifice for him.

'Goodbye,' she said at last, huskily. 'Be happy. Good dog.'

Celia came with them to the door. Francesco came, too, watching her closely, seeing how close she was to weeping. She controlled herself until the door had closed, then she leaned against it, making no effort to hide the tears that now streamed down her face.

'That was a very brave and generous thing you did,' he said gently.

'No, it wasn't. I should have let him go at once. How could I be so cruel as to keep the poor creature here against his will?'

'But you didn't.'

'I was going to be so practical. But I could feel his misery and I couldn't bear it.'

'I'm glad,' he said.

'But just think of the ramifications of this,' she cried.

'It's actually very simple. Tomorrow you contact the society, explain what happened and ask them to find you another dog. In the meantime, just call me Jacko.'

'You know what you've let yourself in for, don't you?'

'And you know that I am willing.'

'I must be crazy.'

'Hey, play fair! Don't keep all the craziness to yourself. I've earned some, too.'

'What are you talking about?' she asked, laughing weakly.

'Well, I know that for you only crazy people count, and I'm doing my best.'

'Oh, *caro,* will I ever understand you?' She sighed.

'Probably not. But you could make me a coffee.'

As they sat in the kitchen he said, 'So, tell me about my duties. Shall I wear a harness?'

Her lips twitched. 'I think I can let you off the harness. But you have to obey my every command. Sit when I say *sit.*'

'Curl up under your chair when you don't need me?'

'I'd love to tell you to do just that,' she mused. 'I think I might just enjoy this. Whether you will is another matter.'

'I've told you—I'm a slave to your every whim. Well, except for one thing. I draw the line at the pooper-scooper.'

She gave a little choke of laughter that enchanted him. 'Hmm! So much for being my slave.'

'I'll be Jacko's substitute in every other way,' he promised. 'I'll even sleep at the foot of your bed.'

'You'll sleep in the spare room like a good doggie,' she told him firmly.

'Wuff!' he said.

CHAPTER NINE

THE next day they drove to the Villa Rinucci to collect his things. Knowing his mother, Francesco took the precaution of telephoning her first, to explain that this was strictly a practical arrangement, and would she kindly refrain from asking Celia when the wedding was going to be?

'*Please,* Mamma—unless you want me to die of embarrassment.'

Hope promised to be good, and contented herself with loading Celia with gifts of home-baked treats, which she received with delight. Then it was back to the apartment for him to unpack and settle into the spare room, where they made the bed together.

As they were preparing a meal she said, 'I called the society. They were very understanding and said they'll find me another dog, but it may take a couple of months. I hope you won't find that awkward.'

'I hope *you* won't,' he said. 'I know you don't want me around that long.'

'We'll just have to try to endure each other,' she said lightly.

The exchange was pleasant enough, but behind it they were each assessing a situation that had taken them by surprise.

They spent the evening working in their various ways.

Francesco had brought his laptop so that he could direct the firm as far as possible.

'Is this going to damage you?' she asked worriedly. 'Your business is only just starting and the boss is deserting it.'

'I can still go in for a few hours. You can come with me. It'll help you assess our progress for your report.'

At last he said, 'Isn't it time for the evening walk? We both need some fresh air.'

Francesco found that he was nervous. Earlier in the day he'd taken her arm for a few moments when they'd visited the villa, but that had been too brief to count. And in the apartment she knew her way around. But this would be the real test—the first time she would be completely reliant on him.

She took his arm as they left the building and went down the three stone steps together.

'Let's head for the docks,' she said. 'Or shall we go the other way and wander around the shops?'

'You're the boss. Isn't that what Jacko would have said?'

'No, he wouldn't, and nor would Wicksy. In many ways they were the boss. Let's head for the port.'

As they walked he asked, 'How was Jacko the boss?'

'If I wanted to cross the road and he could see that it wasn't safe he'd refuse. I'd say, Go forward, and he'd just sit there, sometimes actually on my foot so that I knew he meant business. He could see the danger, so I had to take his advice.'

'Yes, I saw that once or twice,' he recalled. 'I thought he was being awkward.'

'No, he was doing his job. And sometimes he'd obey me in a roundabout way. If I said, Forward, and the way was blocked, he'd go sideways and find a way to negotiate the problem.' She squeezed his arm. 'He was a clever dog. He knew there was more than one way forward.'

'Yes, I guess he did,' Francesco murmured.

They wandered the short distance towards the sea, and she stood breathing in the odours of a busy port.

'That's good,' she said. 'I love the sea.'

He made a non-committal reply and she let it drop, remembering that the sea conjured up unfortunate memories for him.

'Do you want to go in any particular direction?' he asked.

'No, I don't know any details. Jacko was a good guide, but he never told me how things looked.'

After a moment he realised that she had made a joke, but by then it was too late to respond.

'What do you want to know?'

'Tell me about the boats.'

He did so, describing the ferries that came and went while she leaned on the wall that overlooked the water, an expression of total absorption on her face. At last she sighed and reached out for him.

'Let's go,' she said. 'Francesco?'

For a moment she touched only empty air, and she was suddenly full of tension.

'I'm here,' he said, quickly taking her hand. 'Sorry—my mind wandered for a moment.'

'I didn't know where you were,' she said quietly. 'I didn't know where *I* was.'

'I'm sorry,' he said urgently. 'I'm sorry.'

'Don't take it so much to heart,' she told him, smiling faintly.

'You're shivering.'

'I guess it's getting cold. Shall we go?'

He gave a groan.

'I'm useless at this. I thought it would be simple but it isn't. I keep wanting to tell you everything, then backing off in case I overdo it and annoy you.'

For a moment Celia was silent, too shocked to speak. The words, *He's afraid,* flashed through her brain.

From the beginning she'd known him as a forceful, domineering man, easily annoyed with people who wouldn't agree with him, including herself. But with her he'd suppressed his exasperation, always loving and tender, except in their quarrels. Even then she'd sensed him controlling himself, and it had had the perverse effect of increasing her anger because she'd felt she was being patronised. With a sighted woman he'd have felt free to let his anger explode. She'd always been certain of that.

Now she wasn't so sure.

She'd thrown him out, but was that the only reason for his hesitation? Hadn't it always been there, if she'd had the wit to sense it?

He's afraid, she thought again. And hard on the heels of that came the worst thought of all. Afraid of *me.*

'Let's try again,' he said. 'I'm holding out my arm close to you.'

'If you were a gentleman you'd take my hand and tuck it into place,' she said, in a voice that sounded strangely shaky.

'Sure—if that's all right with you.'

She felt him fit her hand into the crook of his elbow, and waited for him to give it a small pat before withdrawing his own hand. But he didn't, and a thousand thoughts clashed in her mind.

Forceful? Domineering? *Him?*

He's on hot coals for fear of offending me. Is that what I've done to him?

'Let's get back,' she said. 'I'm very tired.'

A moment ago she could have walked for ever. Suddenly

she was nervous. A sense of failure was creeping over her. She wasn't used to it and didn't know how to cope.

They walked home in silence.

Sharing an apartment, which had seemed so simple, turned out to be a minefield. Before, they had lived together with the casual intimacy of lovers, free to walk in on each other half dressed, without thinking.

Now he was a cross between an upper servant and a guide dog, with no privileges, only a duty to keep a respectful distance and obey his owner at all times. He had persuaded her on the solemn promise of respecting that duty.

Francesco's first inkling of just how tough this was going to be came on the second evening. Searching for his favourite pen, he recalled that it had been in his jacket pocket the night they had made love. He'd torn the jacket off, tossing it onto the floor. Now the pen was missing, so it had probably fallen onto the floor and might be there still.

Thinking Celia was in the bathroom, he went into her room. But she was sitting on the bed, naked except for a tiny pair of pink satin briefs.

'I'm sorry,' he said hastily, backing off. 'I thought you were— I'll go.'

'Did you want something?'

'I was looking for my—' Maddeningly, he found that his mind was blank. 'Never mind. Another time.'

He got out fast, shocked by what was happening to him. He'd seen her wearing less before—many times—but always with her willing consent. Now he felt like a Peeping Tom, intruding on her vulnerability. Most stunning of all was the undignified thrill of seeing something that should have been off-limits. Illicit pleasure, forbidden enchantment. It was like

watching *What The Butler Saw,* utterly disgraceful and un-
bearably exciting.

He fled to his own room while he still had some self-
control, and lay all night without sleeping.

They found a kind of routine. Within the apartment she
needed no help, because she knew where everything was.
She would cook, and even clean the place, although she
employed help for this. Not because she was blind, but because the success of her work left her little time to spare.

Francesco insisted on looking after himself, including
making his own bed, despite Celia's mischievous insistence
that she had never required this from Jacko.

If she worked at her projects at home he would be free to
leave her for a few hours, to put some time in at his own job.
If she was working with Sandro he would deliver her to
Sandro's office and leave her in his care, collecting her at the
end of the day.

The parachute jump had caused a lot of interest, and
Francesco waited for Celia to announce her own jump. He was
well prepared, his self-control primed and ready for the worst.
When the blow fell he would not protest. He would accept her
decision, drive her to the airfield and muffle his terror.

But days passed with no announcement, and he allowed
himself a sigh of relief.

Last thing at night they would take a walk together through
the streets of Naples, while he described the sights to her. These
were their happiest times. Sometimes they would stand by the
water's edge, listening to the cry of sea-gulls and the sounds
coming from the boats, before walking back to the apartment.

It wasn't exciting, but it was comfortable. He could sense her
relaxing with him, and knew that this was a new phase for them.

One night she said, 'Why do we always branch left here?

Isn't there a right branch that would get us home just as well?
Or have I got that wrong?'

'It would take longer,' he prevaricated.

'I don't care. Let's take the other way.'

'I'll bet you didn't argue with Jacko like this.'

'I wasn't suspicious of Jacko.'

'I'll sit on your foot in a minute,' he threatened.

They laughed together, making their way slowly along the
street until they came to the moment when his dark secret
was revealed.

'Who's that calling us overhead?' she asked.

'That's my brother, Ruggiero,' Francesco said in a resigned
voice. 'He and Polly live in this block, and right now they're
leaning out, enjoying the sight of me being a good dog.'

'But how do they know that's what you're doing?'

'How long do you think it took to go around the family?'
he asked through gritted teeth. 'No, don't stop—let's get on.'

'We can't go without talking to your relatives if they've
seen us. It wouldn't be polite.'

From above them came riotous cries of, 'Woof, woof!'

'Take a running jump,' Francesco called back. 'Preferably
out of that window.'

'Celia, tell your hound to lead you in this direction,'
Ruggiero called down.

'Well, go on,' she told him. 'Good doggie. Obey!'

'I'll get my own back,' he vowed as they went up. But he
was grinning.

'You've been avoiding us,' Ruggiero said when they were
each settled with cake and a glass of white sparkling *prosecco*.

'And you've been looking out for us,' Francesco said.
'Don't tell me you haven't leaned out of the window every
night, hoping for a good laugh at me.'

'All right, I won't say it,' Ruggiero agreed.

Newly married, they had just finished visiting the more far-flung family members. Justin and Evie had welcomed them in England; Luke and Minnie had given them a riotous party in Rome.

'Mind you, most of the riot came from Minnie's previous in-laws,' Polly recalled. 'Heavens, they know how to give a party! We were exhausted when we went on to Uncle Franco and Aunt Lisa the next day. Luckily they're much more sedate, because I don't think we had enough energy for another mad evening.'

'How are they?' Francesco asked.

There was nothing in his voice to suggest that the subject particularly concerned him, and Celia wondered if she only imagined that the casual note was just a little contrived.

'They seem fine,' Ruggiero replied. 'Of course, they're getting old. Aunt Lisa has had bronchitis recently, but she's over it now. And Uncle Franco—well, you know him.'

'Not really,' Francesco said quietly. 'I've seen very little of him.'

Now Celia was sure she heard something strange in his voice. It seemed a good moment to discover that she had a headache, and in a few minutes they were heading home.

For a while she chatted casually, but at last it got through to her that he wasn't responding.

'What is it?' she asked.

'Nothing.'

'It's not like you to be so silent. Has something upset you.'

'You're not the only one with a headache,' he said abruptly. 'Let's get home.'

When the apartment door was locked behind them he bade her good-night as quickly as possible, and she did the same. It wasn't what she wanted. Painful as it was, she had to accept that.

She longed to reach out to him and take his troubles on herself—for that he was in some kind of trouble there could be no doubt.

In the old days she would have enfolded him in her arms and her heart, giving him all her love. But now things had changed, and suddenly she knew she had to be cautious. Like him, she went to bed without delay.

She fell asleep quickly, then awoke in the early hours, certain that some noise had disturbed her, but there was only silence. Sitting up in bed, she listened, and at last heard a muffled sound that seemed to come from next door. Slipping out of bed, she opened her door and went to stand outside Francesco's room. Now she could clearly hear the desperate, gasping mutters from inside.

Turning the handle quietly, she slipped inside and went to the bed. Sitting down on it, she discovered that Francesco was lying on his back, his eyes closed, muttering in his sleep. At first she couldn't make out the words, but then she realised that he was saying the same thing, over and over.

'Get out—get out—get out—'

'Francesco—' She shook him, but he didn't wake. It was as though he was trapped inside his nightmare, with no escape.

'Francesco!'

She shook his shoulders again, but he only began to toss and turn. Moving her hands gently across his face, she discovered that his cheeks were wet, as though he was weeping in his sleep.

She hesitated. They had set rules for sharing the apartment—rules that kept them firmly on different sides of a line. But this situation wasn't covered by any rule that she acknowledged, and if it had been she would have broken it.

She was about to lean down and kiss him when he let out

a cry and shot up in bed, colliding with her so that she almost fell off, and had to hold on to him.

'Francesco, what's the matter? Are you awake?'

'What? What? *Who are you?*' He was shaking her.

'Francesco—it's me—Celia.'

One of the hands holding her disappeared, and she heard the light being switched on. Dismayed, she wondered if his confusion was really so far gone that he had to see her to be sure.

'For pity's sake, what's the matter?' she begged.

'Nothing, I— What are you doing in here?'

'I heard you cry out in your sleep. Then you were muttering over and over to yourself— It sounded like *Get out.*'

She heard his sharp intake of breath.

'You imagined that,' he said in a cold voice. 'It could have been anything.'

'No, it was definitely *Get out* but—'

'*You imagined that.*'

'All right. Maybe I did.'

'Who knows what people say when they have a bad dream? Don't you ever have them?'

'No,' she said simply. 'But if I did I'd come to you and ask you to put your arms around me. Especially if it was bad enough to make me cry.'

She put her hand up to touch his face, but felt him seize it, holding her away from him.

'Don't be absurd,' he snapped. 'I'm not crying.'

She knew better than to argue, but she was full of confusion. She'd never known him in this mood before.

'Go back to bed,' he said. The anger had gone from his voice, but instead there was a quiet implacability that was more daunting.

'Good night,' she said.

If he'd softened for the briefest moment she would have kissed him. But all her senses told her that he was hard as iron, and she left the room.

She lay awake for a long time, listening for any sound from his room, but there was nothing. Everything had changed, she realised. In their old quarrels it had always been him trying to reach out to her, while she withdrew from what she considered his interference. Now it was he shutting her out.

She had not the slightest inkling why it had happened. But she was suddenly afraid.

The following day Celia chose to stay at home, freeing Francesco to leave and concentrate on his factory.

'But if you need me, just call and I'll come home,' he said.

'Don't worry. I shan't be going out,' she replied, as scrupulously polite as he.

'I expect you have your day's work all planned?' he observed.

'Actually, I thought I'd do some cooking.'

She could tell he was surprised, but he said no more, only lay a hand on her shoulder and departed.

Left alone, she didn't immediately get out any ingredients, but pondered for a while, then called Hope.

'I'm practising being a good housewife today,' she told her cheerfully. 'I know some of Francesco's favourite dishes, but only the English ones. I thought you could advise me about the Italian ones.'

'An excellent idea,' Hope said at once. 'Shall I come over?'

'Lovely.'

Hope arrived an hour later to find the coffee already perking. She'd come prepared with home-made cream cakes, and they plunged into a delicious session without delay.

'You don't need Francesco today?' Hope asked, looking around.

'Not while I'm here. I know this place so well that he's only in the way.'

They laughed together.

'Poor Francesco.' Hope sighed. 'He's trying so hard to be useful to you.'

'I wish…' Celia paused. 'I wish I knew what he was really like.'

'You can't tell from being with him?'

'I know how he is with me, but—in a way, we fell in love too soon. We really knew how we felt the first evening. It took us a week to admit the truth, but it was there from the start. I sometimes wish it had taken longer, so that I could have become acquainted with the man he was before.'

'Before love changed him?' Hope said, understanding. 'I'm not sure that I can be much help. I saw little of him for the past ten years.'

'And you don't know what his demons are?'

'Ah, you've discovered those. Do they trouble him at night?'

'Only recently. He has nightmares, and he won't tell me.'

'Nor me,' Hope said sadly. 'I know it's happened since he returned, but as for before that—you probably know better than me.'

'It never happened in England.'

'He is a strange man,' Hope mused. 'Our family life has been full of upheaval. Justin, my eldest son, was the most affected. After him, I think it troubled Francesco most, but in a way I find hard to understand.'

'I've heard Francesco mention Justin. You only found each other a few years ago, didn't you?'

'Yes, he was born when I was only fifteen, and stolen from

me. Luke and Primo were part of my marriage, but
Francesco—well.'

'I'm not trying to pry,' Celia said hurriedly. 'It's none of
my business.'

'But I think I would like to tell you. I've known you only
a short while, yet I feel I can trust you—as I know Francesco
trusts you.'

'You *can* trust me,' Celia assured her.

'When I married my first husband in England, years ago,
he already had a son—Primo—by his first wife, Elsa. She'd
been a Rinucci—Toni's sister. She died, I married Primo's
father, and we adopted Luke. It wasn't a happy marriage, and
that was my fault. I married him for safety, but safety wasn't
enough. Then I met Franco Rinucci. He was Elsa's and
Toni's brother, and he came from Italy to visit Primo. And
so we met.'

She paused, and a heavy silence filled the room.

'And so we met…' she repeated.

Then there was another silence.

'And it happened?' Celia asked softly.

Hope turned to her, smiling through her tears.

'Yes, it happened. We knew in the first moment. We tried
to fight it, for we were both married with children. He stayed
with us for a week, and when he left I was pregnant. We knew
we couldn't be together. I would never have asked him to
leave his wife and children, and he wouldn't have done so.
We had that one week—the most glorious of my life. But
glory doesn't last. It can't. It shouldn't. Nobody could live
on that pinnacle for ever. I shall always have that week, and
I shall always have the child who took his life from that
lovely time.'

'Francesco?'

'Yes, Francesco. For a long time my husband thought the baby was his. He even made a favourite of him. But then he discovered the truth and threw us out. I got custody of Luke, but he kept Primo.

'Soon after that my husband died, and Primo came to Italy to live with the Rinuccis. I came out here to see him, and that was how I met the rest of the family.'

'Including Toni?'

'Oh, yes. He was a fine young man in his thirties—very strong, but very gentle.'

'Did you see Franco on that visit?' Celia asked.

'Briefly. His home was in Rome. He and his wife came down for a short while. I think we had five minutes alone. That was all either of us could have endured. The following day I told Toni that I would marry him.'

'Does he know about you and Franco?'

'I tried to tell him but he silenced me. He said that our lives would begin from that moment, and that nothing that happened before was any of his business.'

'So he suspects but doesn't want to know?' Celia hazarded.

'I think so. He has never asked questions. It's almost deafening, the way he doesn't ask anything.'

'Did you marry him for safety?' Celia asked cautiously.

'I thought I did,' Hope said. 'But then a strange thing happened. I found that I had married a man who was kind and loveable—who gave everything, asked little in return, and always put my happiness before his own. I ask you, what is to be done with such a man?'

'There is only one thing to do with him,' Celia replied at once. 'And that is to love him.'

'That's how I feel, too.'

Warmed by Hope's trust, Celia ventured say, 'But it's not the same as being *in* love, is it?'

Hope didn't answer for a moment, and when she did her eyes were focused on a distant place and her voice was soft.

'As I said, I had my pinnacle and it was glorious.' She was silent a moment. 'Perhaps there is more to life than being in love.'

Perhaps, Celia thought. But at this moment she couldn't believe it.

CHAPTER TEN

FRANCESCO got home late that night. Celia was already in her room, and she heard him moving about quietly, so not to wake her. Once he looked in, but she pretended to be asleep. Anything was better than forcing him to talk to her when he clearly didn't want to.

For the first time she faced the possibility of defeat—something she'd never done in her life before. Right from the start—the child of two blind parents who'd conquered the world, she'd known that failure wasn't an option. Aided by a sharp brain and a natural talent, she'd mastered everything that came her way. It also helped to have a bolshie nature, she acknowledged.

Whatever she wanted, she went out and fought for—sometimes with blunt weapons. All those months ago, when she'd first met Francesco, if he hadn't come to her after the first week she would have sought him out and *made* him understand that they belonged together.

Throwing him out had been an act of recklessness that she'd soon regretted. So she'd made her plans—travelling to a strange country with a smile on her face, challenging all comers. The one she'd challenged the most was Francesco himself. And she'd been winning; her heart and her singing flesh told her that.

Then something had gone wrong, but exactly what it was still mystified her. It had started with his nightmare—No, before that, earlier in the evening, when Minnie had mentioned Aunt Lisa and Uncle Franco, his secret father.

On the pretext of cooking instructions she'd sought help from Francesco's mother, who hadn't been fooled for a moment. The two women had understood each other perfectly, and Celia had learned a good deal. But it didn't explain the dark mood that had suddenly come down over Francesco's mind.

At breakfast the next day she said, 'I had a call from the society yesterday. They think they'll have a dog for me soon. I'll have to go and live there for a month, so that we can get used to each other, but then I'll be all right.'

'Good. You'll feel happier. Let's hope he's as good as Jacko.'

This was how it would be from now on. His manner to her was pleasant and helpful, but no longer charged with something that made the air vibrate.

He performed his guide-dog duties perfectly, but time was moving on. Those duties would soon be over, and their best chance would be lost. She'd thrown the dice and she had failed.

Worst of all was the knowledge that she'd failed in understanding. He wasn't sufficiently at ease with her to open up. That was the truth of it.

It's always been about me, she thought, dismayed. I talk about being exactly like everyone else, but I talk about it too much. When did I ever let the poor man get a word in edgeways? Now it's too late. No, it mustn't be. *It mustn't be!*

But she didn't know what to do.

Every two weeks Hope arranged a family gathering at the villa for anyone who happened to be in Naples at the time. Usually this simply meant those who lived there, but occasionally a distant relative passed through and was scooped up for a dinner party. When Toni's second cousin once removed came to visit, he and his wife were feasted like royalty.

The younger members of the family thought them pleasant, but dull, and were politely relieved when a car arrived to collect them. But Hope and Toni followed them out to say more goodbyes by the car.

'You should go and join them,' Della scolded Carlo. 'Where are your manners?'

'They died a death when he told that story about the boar for the fifth time,' he said faintly.

She aimed a playful swipe at him, but she did him an injustice. A slight family resemblance had made Carlo the object of the old man's attention most of the evening. He'd done his duty with great charm. Now he'd earned a breather.

'You're driving us home tonight, aren't you?' he checked with his wife.

'Promise.'

'In that case I'll have a large whisky,' he said with relief.

When they were all sitting around, relaxing, Celia said, 'Why don't you tell us the rest of *your* story?'

This raised a laugh. For most of the evening Carlo had been trying to tell an anecdote of his own, constantly interrupted by their guest, who had led everything back to his own tale of the boar.

'Right—I'll tell it fast,' Carlo said. 'This man came to the door, and when he—'

He plunged into the story. Francesco watched him, and also Della, who laughed at her husband's story as freely as if she hadn't heard it a dozen times already. They were clearly happy and at ease with each other, he thought, remembering how stressed he'd seen them before.

'I see that you've got it sussed,' Francesco said as Carlo finished the story and came in search of his wife. 'I wish you'd tell me the secret.'

'The strange thing,' Carlo mused, 'is that it was you who told me the secret. Since your warning I've been watching myself—backing off, in case I smother Della with my love. I could end up depriving her of any meaningful life, which would be easier for me but would destroy her.'

'So why can't I practise what I preach?' Francesco sighed in frustration. 'I can't seem to find the way.'

'You won't,' Carlo told him. 'It'll find you. One day you'll just see the path at your feet, and that's when you have to decide whether to walk it. If you walk forward it'll be hard, but she'll be there, waiting. Until then you just have to keep watching for the moment.'

The phone rang in the hall, just outside.

'I'll get it,' Carlo said. 'I'm nearest.'

He vanished into the hall, and they heard him say, 'Ciao, Minnie.'

Celia appeared at Francesco's side, asking, 'Is she the one who lives in Rome, with Luke? Ruggiero and Polly visited them recently?'

'That's right. Minnie's a lawyer and Luke owns an apartment block. They met because she was fighting him on behalf of his tenants. They started by going at it hammer and tongs and ended up married.'

'Hammer and tongs can make a very good beginning,' Celia said. 'You discover the worst of the other person, and if you can fall in love after that you have real hope.'

There was a general laugh at this, then Primo said, 'Just a minute— I think something's wrong. Carlo's voice has changed.'

They all grew alert, and heard Carlo say, 'All right. I'll get Poppa.'

By this time Toni and Hope had finished their goodbyes and were returning to the house, just as Carlo appeared, saying urgently, 'Luke's on the phone. Aunt Lisa is very ill.'

Toni and Hope hurried to the phone at once.

'It's bad, then?' Primo asked.

'She's dying,' Carlo said. 'She had a massive heart attack, and the doctors say there's very little hope. Uncle Franco asked Luke to call us, because he can't leave her for a moment.'

There were murmurs of consternation. Most of the others rose and surrounded Carlo, asking him questions, but Della remained with Celia, saying, 'They live in Rome, so Luke and Minnie have seen more of them than the rest of us. It's strange, really. Rome isn't so far away, but they never seem to join us here for family celebrations.'

Remembering what Hope had told her, Celia realised this wasn't surprising. The love between her and Franco had been so strong that they had to avoid each other—even years later. Now Franco's wife would soon be dead. His children were grown, and he would a free man. How would this make her feel? And Toni? Would he be afraid lest this changed everything?

At last Hope and Toni returned.

'How bad is it?' everyone asked.

'She's going,' Toni said heavily. 'My brother wants his family there.'

There were murmurs of agreement from the others, but Francesco said, 'I can't come, Mamma. I can't leave Celia alone.'

He spoke in a low voice, but Celia heard him—and Hope's immediate response. 'I hope Celia will come with us. I regard her as one of the family.'

'Thank you,' she said. 'I'll be glad to come.'

Inwardly she thought that there was more here than met the eye, but she, who had no eyes, might see more clearly than the others. Concern for her was chiefly an excuse. Francesco had his own reasons for not wanting to visit his true father.

It was decided that they would all leave by train the next day. An invitation to stay at Franco's home was politely refused.

'He will have enough on his mind without playing host to all of us,' Hope declared. 'There are several good hotels.'

After that the party broke up, and they made arrangements to meet at the railway station in the morning. For once Celia wished she could see. Hope had trusted her with her feelings, and now she would have liked to seek her out and speak to her. But it would attract too much attention.

She had to settle for asking Francesco to take her to his mother and giving her a hug. Through the pressure of the older woman's arms she sensed the feelings Hope could not express.

Francesco didn't speak until they were home, and then he said awkwardly, 'I'm afraid you were rather corralled into that, whether you like it or not.'

'I'm happy to come. If only I thought you wanted me there.'

'Nonsense—why shouldn't I?' He sounded edgy.

'Because there's something about this that you're keeping to yourself. There are warning signs all around you, telling me to keep off.'

'You're imagining that,' he said impatiently. 'If I'm a little awkward it's because of something I have to tell you. Della booked the hotel rooms, and she automatically booked each couple into a double room. I couldn't think of a way to tell her that we didn't want that, but when we get there I'll change it.'

'No, don't do that. In strange surroundings I'll be safer in the same room with you. Leave things as they are.'

'That's fine, then.' He stopped, as though words suddenly came hard to him.

She turned her head in his direction, trying to read the silence. She'd always been able to do so before, but this time he was blocking her out. The nothingness that resulted was the most frightening thing that had ever happened to her.

But she had to know the truth. If he'd turned against her she needed to feel that, too, by touching him, experiencing his bitterness through her fingers.

Celia began to walk in his direction, moving slowly and quietly, not to alert him. That was how she discovered that he was sitting down, his head sunk low, as though he'd come to the end of something and didn't know what to do next. Aghast at her own stupidity, she realised that there was no hostility here, only a dismal despair, bleak and all-engulfing.

'Tell me what it is,' she begged, leaning over him from behind and putting her arms around him.

'I can't,' he said in a stony voice. 'I don't know.'

'How can you not know what's troubling you? You didn't have these dark moods before.'

'Sometimes I did—they've always come over me without warning, all my life. But not very often, so it wasn't a problem. They'd come and then they'd go, sometimes for years. I thought I'd got the better of them for good. But suddenly they came back, all in a rush, a few months ago.'

'Because of me?'

'It's connected with you,' he said reluctantly, 'but not only you. There's something else—like a huge shadow looming over me, blotting out everything else.'

'I know about Franco,' she said softly. 'Your mother told me.'

'That he's my father? Yes, it's one of those things that everyone knows and nobody mentions, for Toni's sake. But it isn't a big deal, funnily enough. We've only met a few times. When we do, we look each other over, exchange the time of day, and that's that. I don't look like him, luckily, and he has another son and two daughters. I've always been content to leave it like that. Toni's been a great father to me, and I wouldn't hurt him for the world.'

Before she could say any more he added quickly, 'It's getting late, and we need to make an early start tomorrow.'

They went to their separate rooms for the night. Celia lay listening carefully for any sound from Francesco. But all was quiet, which meant that either the nightmare hadn't returned or he, too, was lying awake, determined not to sleep and give himself away.

Celia was a little reluctant when they set out for Naples Central Railway Station next morning. This was a family occasion, and she didn't really belong, yet a part of her wanted to be with Francesco—to be ready for whatever might happen. Perhaps she could be of no help to him. Perhaps he would shut her out. But he was going to need her in some way, of that she was certain.

In less than two hours they were drawing into Rome Central, where cars waited to take them to the hotel. The room she shared with Francesco overlooked the Via Veneto. It was large, and had two double beds, and through the windows came sounds from the luxurious heart of the city.

Celia declined the chance to go to the hospital with the rest.

'I've got a headache,' she said untruthfully to Francesco. 'We'll meet up later.'

Alone, she unpacked and walked the room to get a mental picture of it. She'd taken the precaution of bringing some work with her, and spent the next hour listening to tapes and dictating messages. But it was a relief when her cellphone rang and she found herself talking to Sandro.

'How long will you be away?' he asked. 'Things are beginning to happen here.'

She explained the position and he sighed.

'I guess you'll do what you have to do. But why you're taking the trouble for that prickly, awkward so-and-so I'll never know.'

'That's easy,' she said. 'It's *because* he's a prickly, awkward so-and-so. He needs me.'

'*I* need you.'

'No, you don't. You've got your life together in a way he'll never have.'

Sandro chuckled. 'Well, don't tell *him* that. He'd never forgive either of us. He hates my guts. The two times we met, the air was full of it.'

'He's afraid you're going to talk me into doing a jump.'

'Talk you— You're the one who found that place, remember? And we had a fight about who was going to make the first jump. You were ready to murder me when I won.'

'Well, there's no need to go into that,' she said hastily. 'It's best forgotten.'

'That's a pity, because the press are dead keen for you to do it. Simon wants you to call him. He writes for *L'Esperienza*.'

Her heart gave a leap before she had time to think. But then—

'I can't even think of it just now.'

'Of course. Just make the call and say you'll do it when you can. The number is—'

'I've got his number. I have to go now.'

She hung up and lay back on the bed, thoughtful. After a moment she switched her cellphone off.

There was a knock on the door.

'It's me,' Della called. 'And I've got goodies—tea and cakes.'

'I could kill for a cup of tea,' Celia said, opening the door.

When they were seated, and enjoying the first cup, Della gave a long sigh and said, 'I took the chance to get away. It's really the sons who belong with Franco, not us. Francesco really needs to be there. I think he's feeling a bit edgy.'

'What's Uncle Franco like? He said there was no resemblance.'

'There isn't. They're both tall, but that's about it. Uncle Franco is hefty and muscular, like a football player, and he's managed to keep his figure without putting on weight.'

'I wonder what Hope thinks of him now,' Celia mused.

'She's not giving anything away. I was watching her, so elegant and proper, everything in its place, the perfect picture of a respectable, virtuous, elderly matron. And I suddenly realised what an eventful life she's had. Her first child at fifteen, then a husband, a lover, another child, then another husband. The rest of us are quite dull by comparison. Even now, Hope is still beautiful, but I've seen pictures of her as a young woman, and in those days she was more than beautiful. She had a sort of wild quality that makes it clear why all the men fell for her.'

'There's a wedding picture of her and Toni. She's smiling at the camera, but he's looking at her with his heart in his eyes. It's been there ever since, according to Carlo. He says all the time they were growing up they knew that if Toni said, "That's how Mamma wants it," then that was how it was going to be.'

'But aren't we making too much of this?' Celia asked. 'Maybe Franco *was* the great love of her life, but that was years ago. She's not going to leave Toni now.'

'No, but if he senses that the old feeling is still there between them it will hurt him terribly. She's everything to him. He's such a dear, I'd hate him to be hurt.'

'So would I,' Celia said. 'Even though I don't know what he looks like, every time he's there I get a feeling of kindness and gentle strength.'

'That's Toni,' Della agreed.

Everyone returned from the hospital that evening. They had seen Franco, who'd thanked them for coming, but Lisa had failed to regain consciousness, against all their hopes.

Francesco said little, but as they all sat at dinner that evening Celia felt him touch her gently now and then, as though seeking reassurance. She looked forward to the moment when they would be alone together later that night, and she could ask him to confide in her.

But before that there was a phone call that changed everything.

It came just as the meal was ending. Hope answered her cellphone, listened for a moment, then said tersely, 'Very well. I'm coming.'

'What's happened?' Toni asked her.

'Lisa is awake and wants to see us.'

'All of us?' Toni asked softly.

'Me—and Francesco.'

Nobody could have told from Toni's face that this meant anything unusual to him.

'Come with me,' Hope begged.

'No, *cara*. I have no place in this. I'll wait for you here.'

'But—'

'Go,' he said, with sudden intensity.

Hope didn't reply, but she put her arms about her husband and kissed him.

'Francesco,' Toni said in a low voice, 'go with your mother.'

'Yes, Poppa.'

His hand was tight on Celia's. He didn't ask her to accompany him, but neither did he release his grip. They went out to the car together.

Franco met them in the corridor outside his wife's room.

'Lisa is conscious,' he told Hope, 'and she has something she wishes to say—to ask you. All these years it's been on her mind. I've tried to—' He lapsed into the helpless silence of confusion.

'What have you told her?' Hope asked.

'I've denied it,' he said heavily. 'But nothing I say seems to bring her peace.'

'And that's the only thing that matters. Say whatever you have to, Mamma.'

It was Francesco who had spoken, making the others stare at him.

'What do you mean?' Hope asked.

'You know exactly what I mean. Aunt Lisa is dying. Help her.'

Celia heard the click as the door opened, and the faint sound of Hope's footsteps, then a faint, husky voice from within the room. She waited, expecting either that Francesco would lead her forward or that the door would close, shutting her out. Neither happened. By accident or design Hope had forgotten to shut the door.

Lisa's eyes were open as Hope moved quietly towards the bed, and she managed a faint smile.

'Thank you for coming,' she said. 'There's something I need to know. I always lacked the courage before.'

'I understand,' Hope said softly.

'It's about Francesco— Is he—is he Franco's son?'

Francesco, standing in the doorway, saw his mother raise her head and look directly at Franco on the other side of the bed.

'Tell me,' Lisa said weakly. 'I must know before I die.'

At last Hope spoke.

'My dear, I wish you'd asked me years ago, then I could

have told you that it's not true. Francesco isn't his son. I've never told anyone his father's identity, but I never meant to cause you a moment's unease. You should never have doubted Franco. You are everything to him, just as my Toni is everything to me. Now I will leave you.'

She gave Lisa a brief kiss on the cheek and backed out of the room. Her last view was of Franco in his wife's arms. This time she closed the door.

'Mamma,' Francesco said, putting his arm around her, 'was it very hard?'

'I said what had to be said,' Hope told him. 'Giving her peace was all that mattered. You were right about that.'

'It was a good lie,' Francesco said.

Hope gave a little smile.

'Not everything I said was a lie. All those years ago he stayed with her because she was his true love. *She* was. Not me.'

'And the other thing?' he wanted to know. 'About Toni?'

Hope didn't answer in words, but her gaze went over Francesco's shoulder, so that he turned and saw what she had seen. The next moment Hope had gone.

'What's happening?' Celia asked.

'It's Toni,' Francesco told her. 'He came after all. He's been sitting at the end of the corridor.'

'Where he could be there for Hope but not intrude on her,' she said.

'Yes, I think so. But now she's walking towards him. He's seen her—he's got to his feet—she's started to run—he's opened his arms to her and—'

'Let's go,' Celia said softly. 'There are some things that nobody's eyes should see.'

CHAPTER ELEVEN

IT WAS the early hours of the morning when they arrived back at the hotel. Francesco had been silent since they'd left the hospital, but Celia sensed that it wasn't the same silence as before. She no longer felt shut out from his thoughts. Rather he was immersed in them, struggling to find a way out, but his continual clasp on her hand told her that she was part of everything going on inside him.

Since the beds were so large she hoped he might be tempted to join her, but he slipped quietly into his own. She came to sit by him and said a soft, 'Good night.' He didn't answer, and actually turned away, but before doing so he raised her hand to his lips.

They had slept barely an hour when she was woken by the sound of his voice. She was alert in an instant, slipping out of bed and going to sit beside him, listening for the old cry of, 'Get out.'

But it didn't come. Instead, he was muttering feverishly, 'What did I do? What did I do?' Over and over again the words poured out, intense, anguished.

'*Caro,*' she said, shaking him gently. 'Wake up. It's me.'

She reached out, touching him, running her fingers over his

face. He seized her hands, holding them tight against him, but still he seemed unable to wake.

'Why?' he cried. 'Tell me why? What did I do?'

Driven by desperation, she moved until she was close to his ear and said firmly, 'You didn't do anything. It's not your fault—not your fault.'

She repeated the words like a mantra, with no idea of their meaning, desperately hoping that she'd found the key to whatever tormented him. At first she thought it was hopeless, but gradually his voice slowed, the words became less frantic, but imbued with a kind of despairing resignation.

'It's not your fault,' Celia repeated.

'Yes, it is—it was something I did—or why did he throw us out? Why? *Why?*'

Briefly she wondered if it was their own quarrel and its aftermath that tormented him, but he'd spoken of 'he' and 'us.'

She gave him a shake, determined to wake him because she didn't think he could bear this any longer. But instead of waking he began to mutter, 'Get out, get out, get out—'

'Wake up!' she cried. 'Francesco, please wake up.'

Suddenly he went still in her hands, and the sound of his gasp told her that he was awake.

'What are you doing here?' he whispered.

'I'm always here. Whenever you want me. Francesco, tell me what happened. You kept saying, *What did I do?* And then you started saying "Get out" again. What was your dream?'

'It was more than a dream,' he groaned. 'It was all happening again, just like last time.'

'Tell me quickly, while you can still remember. Why do you say, "Get out"? Did I give you the nightmare, by saying that when we quarrelled?'

'Not really. You triggered it with those words, but it goes

back long before you. Only I couldn't remember. That's what was so terrible. It was always there, waiting to come back, but I couldn't see it or confront it.'

'But tonight—'

'Yes, tonight he came back. As he's been waiting to do for years.'

'He? Who is he? Is he a real man, or did you imagine him?'

'He was real once. He's been dead for years, but to me he'll always be real.'

'What happens in the dream?'

'He towers over me,' Francesco said hoarsely. 'So high he seems almost to reach the ceiling. He looks like a giant because I'm only three years old. I'm terrified of him, and I want to run away, but I don't because only cowards run. He taught me that. He taught me lots of things—we were so close. I learned everything he had to teach. I thought he was wonderful.'

'But who was he?'

'His name was Jack Cayman—Mamma's first husband, the man I once thought was my father. I can see him, leaning down to me—I couldn't take my eyes off him—and screaming, "*Get out! And take this little bastard with you.*"'

Celia held him tightly. 'Go on,' she urged.

'He just screamed, "*Get out, get out!*" again and again. I didn't know what he meant, or what had happened, but I know we left the same day. He must have found out the truth—that he wasn't my father.'

'You said you were close?'

'Yes, he made a favourite of me. The joke is that he used to say that of us three boys I was the one most like him. Luke was adopted, Primo was his own son, but for some reason he latched on to me as the kind of son he truly wanted. I loved that. The best thing in the world was when he swept me up in his arms, tossed me the air, then caught me, grinning all over his face. I guess I was a bit of a chauvinist, like boys of three tend to be. Mamma came in handy at feeding time, but the one who mattered was my dad. His love, his approval—they were what made the sun come out.

'Then suddenly, in one hour, it was all taken away. And I didn't know what I'd done wrong. I just knew that warmth and safety had vanished without warning, leaving a terrible emptiness.'

'Poor little boy,' she mourned.

'Of course, I learned the details later. He was livid because he'd found out that he wasn't my father, and it wasn't anything *I'd* done, but it was too late to make any difference, and what happened that night got blotted out. All I knew was that the words *Get out* always had a strange impression on me. If I heard them, it was as though a switch had been thrown.'

'But surely you didn't hear them often? How many people would dare tell *you* to get out?'

He gave a faint bark of laughter. 'One or two have tried. There was one lady who was so determined to be rid of me that my feet barely touched the floor.'

'She sounds like a very stupid woman to me,' Celia said, lying down beside him, her face close to his.

'No, she was a very clever one. I realised that she was right when I got over my shock enough to do some thinking. I've always been a bit forceful, and nobody had really stood up to me before, you see. But it wasn't just real people. If I was watching television and one character told another to get out the words triggered something in my mind. And I'd be in a black mood for hours, without understanding why. But it passed, and I'd forget again.'

'But then I screamed the words at you, just like him?'

'Yes, and that's when it really began to haunt me. Because it was actually aimed at me. But it was more than that. It was losing you. Everything that I treasured—warmth, safety, love—had vanished again, leaving me stranded in a desert. And then tonight—coming here, seeing Franco, everything they talked about—it came back. Suddenly I could remember everything that happened that night, and the last brick slipped into place.'

'What happens now?' she asked anxiously.

'It'll be all right now. I can cope because I can confront it.' He turned his face to her on the pillow. 'Mind you, I'm never going to be sweetness and light.'

'Well, I guess I knew that,' she said, snuggling contentedly against him. 'But you know me—I like to live dangerously.'

'You don't want sweetness and light?'

'Bor—ing!' she sang out. 'Bor—ing!'

He felt for her. 'Why are you lying outside the duvet?' he asked.

She scrambled under the covers. 'Is that better?'

'You're still overdressed.'

'So are you.'

They solved the problem at once, not disrobing slowly, to tease, but quickly, like people who couldn't wait to get to their destination. They urgently wanted to be naked together, and when they were they lost no time seeking the moment of complete fulfilment. There would be time for tenderness later. This was important.

For Celia it was almost like making love to a different man. He didn't need to tell her that his shadows had begun to fall away; she could sense it in every movement. But she knew, too, that he needed her presence to escape them completely.

Afterwards they lay together in sleepy contentment, until she said, 'How lovely that Toni came to the hospital.'

'He was bound to. It was always there in the way his eyes followed Mamma around.'

After a moment, he said, speaking hesitantly, 'To be honest, that's the only thing I mind about you being blind. I'll never know if your eyes would have followed me.'

'Then you haven't been looking properly,' she said. 'Because they do—all the time.'

They went to the hospital next day, to hear the news that they had expected.

'She fell asleep finally about an hour ago,' Franco said in a slightly unsteady voice. 'She was conscious almost until the end, and I was able to tell her how much I loved her.'

'She had no real cause to doubt your love,' Hope said gently. 'And in her heart I think she really knew that. You were together for such a long time—nearly forty years.'

Long ago, when they were young and their passion had been at its height, they could have been together. But he had chosen to stay with his wife. The truth behind that choice was there now, as they stood there in the hospital corridor, the slanted sunbeams from the windows falling on their white hair.

As they walked away afterwards Della fell in beside Celia, taking her arm so that Francesco could give his attention to his parents.

'For a man in his sixties Franco's incredibly handsome,' she said in low voice, not to attract attention. 'He must have been dazzling when he was young. Toni's delightful, but I doubt if he was ever dazzling.'

'It's got nothing to do with a man's looks,' Celia told her. 'If it had, I could never fall in love.'

'And you are in love, aren't you?'

'Oh, yes,' Celia murmured. 'Yes, I am.'

'Is everything all right with you and Francesco?'

'It's getting better, but we've a way to go yet.'

Toni had remained behind to talk to his brother, and Francesco took the chance to draw his mother's arm through his and say, 'Is it all right, Mamma? You know what I mean.'

'Yes, all is well, my son. I knew years ago that he loved Lisa more than he loved me. So when he offered to stay with me I told him no.'

'He did offer?'

'Oh, yes. But I knew I must not accept. If he'd left Lisa for me he wouldn't have forgiven me in the long run. Not just because of his children, but also because she was his true love.'

She gave his arm a slight pressure.

'Sometimes the only way you can show how much you love someone is to let them go.'

Lisa's funeral was held three days later. The whole family was there to see her coffin, covered with flowers, being laid to rest. Despite what Celia had said, Della couldn't help wondering what Hope was feeling now. Had the past come back to her, making her heart ache with its loss? Had Franco, too, become sharply aware of what had come and gone?

But Franco's eyes were fixed unwaveringly on the coffin, and his expression was heart-rending. Della stole a glance at Hope, but Hope was looking at Toni.

On the surface life went on as before. The society apologised that Celia's new dog would not be ready as soon as hoped, but Francesco seemed untroubled by the delay.

Things had reached a strange pass between them. They were lovers again, spending nights in each other's arms, just as in the past, yet they never spoke of the future, and an air of impermanence hung over them. There were still decisions to be made, but neither of them wanted to face them for a while.

'We're cowards,' she murmured dozily one night, from the shelter of his arms.

'What's wrong with that?' he wanted to know. 'We've tried being brave, and nuts to it.'

She giggled and blissfully snuggled down farther. The big problems still lurked outside the tent, but in the meantime there was a lot to be said for cowardice.

She supposed it was a sign of losing her nerve that she often kept her cellphone turned off, lest the call come from *L'Esperienza,* demanding that she make her dive from a helicopter. She owed it to the firm that she'd promised to support, but she didn't want to face that decision yet. Eventually she would feel guilty and turn it on again.

In the end the decision was taken out of her hands, when she slipped up to the flat above to return a CD, assuring Francesco that she could manage that little distance alone. It was half an hour before she returned, having got caught up in cheerful gossip.

'There was a phone call for you,' Francesco informed her. A journalist wanting to know when you'd be ready to go skydiving. He says he has a space in the paper all ready, and it can be a good story, but it has to be you, not Sandro.'

'What did you tell him?' she asked.

'I told him I thought you were free any time, and you'd call back tonight to fix the date.'

Astonishment held her silent, staring.

'*You* told him I'd go skydiving?' she echoed in disbelief.

'Yes—and could you call him back quickly? Because he's going out, and he wants to get it settled.'

He left the room abruptly, before his resolve weakened and he said what he really thought—that she must commit herself quickly before he broke down and begged her not to do it.

It was his mother who had given him the clue, saying, 'Sometimes the only way you can show how much you love someone is to let them go.'

He'd heard the words without truly realising what they meant. Now he discovered the reality for himself, and it was terrible. Sweat stood out on his brow, and he had to call on all his stubbornness.

Stubbornness had never failed him before, he thought wryly.

After a while she came to find him.

'Is it all settled?' he asked with forced brightness.

'Yes, I'm going tomorrow. But, Francesco, did you mean it?'

He managed a laugh. 'It's a bit late if I didn't.'

'But why?'

'Does it matter why? I won't fight you any more about anything you want to do. I give in. Do what you feel you must. I'll see things your way.' He added with light irony, 'You'll observe that I make better jokes about it these days.'

She wanted to cry out a protest at the pain she could sense beneath the wit. She didn't want him to give in. That wasn't his way. But neither did she know how she *did* want it to happen.

He increased her discomfiture a moment later when he said, 'All those years of watching Toni with Hope have taught me a few things about graceful yielding.'

'No,' she said at once. 'Not like that. You're not Toni. He's happy that way, but you never could be.'

'You know your trouble?' he said. 'You don't know how to accept winning.'

'But—'

'I'm hungry. How about something to eat?'

Francesco made it impossible for her to pursue the subject. Only when they were getting ready for bed did he say, 'You can send your driver for tomorrow away. I'll take you to the airfield myself.'

'Is that really a good idea?'

'You mean, you don't trust me?' he asked, as lightly as he could manage. 'You think I'll back off at the last minute?'

She had briefly wondered. But while she sought for an answer, he said softly, 'I think I've earned better than that by now.'

'Oh, darling!' She reached for him. 'I'm sorry. I didn't really mean to suggest—'

'Yes, you did,' he said without resentment. 'You always do. And maybe I deserved it once. But I've learned a lot. The trouble is, I don't think you've noticed.'

'Yes, I—' She stopped as the truth of this hit her. She *had* noticed how much easier it was to relax with him these days, but only in a vague way. Preoccupied with herself, she had missed much that she should have seen.

'Never mind,' he said, drawing her close. 'I'll drive you down there tomorrow—if I may?'

'I'd love you to come—if you're sure you won't get too upset.'

'I won't make any trouble,' he said, interpreting her correctly.

Celia kissed him again and again, full of contrition and love and something that was more than either. She didn't understand it at first, but then she sensed his heart beating against hers, so close together that it was one beat. And suddenly she felt everything that he was feeling—sadness, dread, the fear of losing her, but most of all the fear of offending her.

Pain for him was so intense that it almost deprived her of the power of speech. She could only murmur, 'Darling, darling…'

But words weren't enough. Only actions could express the depth of her love, and she tried to show him with ardour and tenderness.

That night their lovemaking was like never before. It was as though they were open to each other in new ways, speaking silently of secrets never shared.

The first time they had loved had been a night of discovery as they'd explored each other's bodies and hearts. Now it was as though they were discovering each other again, with new intensity and sweetness, but also with a new knowledge that cast doubt over the future. The time was coming when a final decision must be made, and the thought of what that decision might be made every movement and caress mean a thousand times more.

When at last they lay quietly together, he whispered, 'Promise to come back to me—until the next time.'

So he understood about the next time, and recognised that it was inevitable, she thought. That should be a help, but mysteriously it was a new source of pain.

'Of course I'll come back,' she said. 'I always do.'

He didn't answer, and she reached out to caress his face, relishing the details, the high forehead and the strong jaw, the mouth with its unexpected sensitivity.

'Darling?' she murmured. 'Darling?'

Then she realised that he had gone to sleep, his arms still about her, and she felt a curious sense of delight.

'It's all right,' she whispered. 'Just stay there. I'll take care of you.'

She stroked his hair, relishing its springy feel in her hands, wondering at the surge of protectiveness that went through her.

Blind in one way, blind in another, she thought, condemning herself. If you can't see other people it's easy to forget their needs.

It would have been so easy to do the dramatic thing and tell him that she had changed her mind and would stay safely on the ground. But she knew she couldn't do that. All her life she'd fought for her precious independence, wounding herself in the process, but never until now seeing the wounds of others. Even now something that was essential to her true self wouldn't let her yield, though he'd generously shown her the way by yielding first. That was the truth of it.

And yet something had changed. Now she understood how much he was in her hands, how cruelly she could make him suffer—far more than he could ever inflict on her.

She leaned down, kissing him gently, not to awaken him.

'Forgive me,' she whispered. 'Forgive me for what I can't help.'

CHAPTER TWELVE

As THEY drove to the airfield next morning Francesco asked lightly, 'Why are you and Mamma thick as thieves these days?'

'Not just us. Olympia and Polly, too, and Della, when she's here instead of hunting backgrounds for her series. There's a big party to be planned for the wedding anniversary.'

'I'd forgotten. How many years is it?'

'Thirty-five. Hope says she and Toni always celebrate in style, but this year it's going to be special. It's all being planned well in advance, so that everyone has time to get here, wherever in the world they live. It's going to be the party to end all parties.'

He thought, but didn't say, Let's hope you're still alive to be there.

But she could read his thoughts. 'And I'm going to be there, too. I've promised Hope that when this jump is over I'll concentrate on the party. You know, it's lovely the way she's welcomed me into the family. In fact, they all have.'

'Maybe they're trying to tell you something.'

'Maybe. I know they've turned this jump into a family occasion. Hope and Toni are going to be there, also Carlo and Della, and maybe some of the others.'

When they reached the airfield Francesco dropped Celia

by the steps into the main building and gave her into the hands of a young woman who would help her change. When she had gone inside he turned to find Carlo and Della approaching him. With his new sharp eyes Francesco saw how Carlo had his arm protectively around Della's shoulders, but so lightly that she wouldn't feel it as a constraint.

'Are you all right?' Carlo asked, giving him a meaningful glance.

Francesco grimaced. 'Surviving.'

'She'll be fine,' Della told him. 'Women are a lot tougher than men allow for. In fact, the truth is that we're a lot tougher than men, full-stop. Isn't that so, *caro?*'

'Yes, dear,' Carlo said in a comically robotic voice. 'No, dear. Anything you say, dear.'

'You two are turning into Mamma and Poppa,' Francesco observed.

Carlo grinned, not in the least offended by the comparison. He drew his wife closer and dropped a swift kiss on the top of her head.

'I've got him well trained.' Della chuckled. 'You'd better watch out. Celia will have you in line in no time.'

'She already has, or we wouldn't be here,' Carlo said. 'Francesco, we'll see you later.'

They wandered off, arms entwined.

Francesco watched them, wondering if he and Celia would ever reach such a pitch of perfect understanding. Or would today be the end of everything, one way or another?

Then he saw the door open and Sandro come out, led by his dog, with Celia's hand tucked in his arm. He brought her over, followed by a man dressed in the same kind of gear Celia was wearing. Relieved, Francesco recognised Sandro's skydiving partner from the previous occasion.

'Just dropped by to tell you not to worry,' he told Francesco. 'Celia and I will jump out together, and I won't let her go until I know she's safe.'

'Who's worried?' Francesco said cheerfully. 'But, thanks.'

'We'll be back for you in a few minutes,' Sandro told Celia, and the two men departed discreetly.

'Everything all right?' Francesco asked. He did his best to sound cheerful, but he could hear the strain in his own voice and doubted he was enough of an actor to hide it.

'Everything's fine,' she said, sounding too polite, too cautious. She was making allowances in case he backed off.

He grew frantic. He *must* convince her that he was really behind her in this. It had never been as important as now.

'That huge thing on your back is your parachute?' he said, putting as much interest in his voice as possible. 'How do you open it?'

'This ring, here—in the front. I just pull it and the parachute opens.'

Suppose it didn't open? It might not and then she'd crash to earth and die. He must stop this madness, for her sake.

But the desperate thoughts that screamed through his head stayed silent on the outside. Instead, he asked brightly, 'What about the other bits and pieces? There are too many to count.'

'This is my two-way radio, so that someone on the ground can warn me if I look like I'm coming down in the wrong place. I can guide the parachute in different directions using these rings. And don't worry—I know exactly where they are and can find them easily.'

'I'm sure of it,' he managed to say.

She laughed then in delight, putting her hand up against his face.

'I love you,' she said.

He took her hand and kissed the palm. 'Come back to me, Celia.'

'But I did,' she said.

'No, I mean—'

'Oh, you can be so stupid sometimes,' she breathed. 'I *did* come back to you. Didn't you notice?'

'You mean—when you came to Naples—it was really— All that stuff you said— You returned to *me?*'

'At last the truth gets through,' she said fondly. 'It took long enough.'

'I've always wondered, but you never exactly—'

'I have to be going now,' she said. 'I love you.'

He kissed her palm again, horribly conscious of Sandro, who had reappeared nearby.

'I love you,' he said quietly. 'Now you must come back to me again—or what shall I do?'

'Time to be going,' Sandro called.

She drew back from Francesco, letting Sandro take her away in the direction of the light plane.

'Come back to me,' Francesco called. *'Come back to me.'*

He waited for her to respond to the sound by turning her head, but she didn't. It was as though everything in her was focused on what would happen next. The last few moments might never have been. He wondered now if she even remembered that he existed.

In fact, he did her an injustice. In her usual methodical way Celia was trying to order him out of her mind, so that she could concentrate on what was about to happen. But his ghost, so tractable before, had become rebellious. It insisted on staying with her every step across the tarmac, reminding her that he existed, and that if she died he still had to find a way to go on existing, however empty it might be.

Now she was at the helicopter, and a hand was reaching out to pull her aboard.

'Good luck!' Sandro said from the ground.

'Thanks,' she replied mechanically.

She heard the door slam, cutting off all sound from outside. Now the only sound was the crackling of the radio and a disembodied voice that came from some mysterious other place.

Come back to me.

Her diving partner touched her shoulder to check all was OK.

She'd met him before, a strong hearty type called Silvio, whose geniality made him pleasant company. She nodded, strapping herself in.

He did a quick check to make sure she'd done it right, and pronounced himself satisfied.

'Check your radio,' he said.

She exchanged a few words with her guide on the ground, and found that everything was working perfectly.

Silvio clapped the pilot on the shoulder to indicate that they were ready.

The whine of the engine that had been in the background now grew higher. Above them the blades whirred, and suddenly they were whisked up into the air, going higher and higher at an incredible speed.

At first her stomach seemed to be falling away from her, but then it steadied itself and she was calm again.

Now Silvio's voice reached her on the radio.

'It'll take us a few minutes to reach our height, then we'll circle a couple of times and return in this direction, so that we can make the jump and land on the airfield, where all your friends can see you.'

'See me make a fool of myself, you mean,' she said lightly. 'With my luck I'll land on the control tower.'

'Nah, that hasn't happened for ages—at least six weeks,' he clowned.

She chuckled. This was how she liked her adventures to be—light-hearted and relaxed.

But the silent companion in her head was reproachful, reminding her that it was *his* life she was dicing with, as well as her own.

'Getting near,' Silvio said. 'I'm about to touch the button that will slide the door back, then I'll jump, taking you with me. When we've jumped, we'll hold on to each other with both hands as we start the fall. Then we'll release hands and pull the rings to release our parachutes.'

'Nearly ready,' said her guide from the ground. 'Helicopter just coming into sight. All set?'

'All set?' Silvio asked her.

'All set,' Celia confirmed.

She felt Silvio's hand tighten on hers, drawing her to the open door.

'Now,' he said.

A sudden pull and they were both free in the air. He seized her other hand and they began to float down, both at full stretch, supported on a blanket of air.

This was when it should happen—the feeling of glorious escape that always came as she launched herself into the unknown. This was her freedom.

But it didn't happen.

'All right?' Silvio asked through the radio.

'Wonderful!'

Silvio released her hands. Now—now it would come. The exhilarating sense of liberation, the thing she lived for. *Now!*

But no rush of joy possessed her. Instead, she realised that the wind was roaring past her, and it was time to pull the ring that would open her parachute.

She yanked, and felt the tug at her back as the parachute streamed up behind her.

'Yeee-haaah!' she cried up into the void.

It was good to be floating down through the fierce, blustering air, and perhaps if she shouted her joy aloud she would recapture the joyous freedom that had always possessed her before.

But then she had an alarming sensation, as though someone had seized her and was throwing her around the sky.

'What's happened?' she cried.

'The wind has changed course,' Silvio told her. 'Don't worry. Pull the upper left ring and you'll turn.'

She scrabbled for the ring, but the wind was fierce on her fingers, making it hard to take hold. She managed it at last, and felt her body swing in the other direction.

'Pull the lower left ring,' Silvio told her. 'It'll help you navigate.'

This time she managed better, and felt the parachute respond. Even so, she wasn't safe yet. She knew that. It was going to take all her cool head to avoid a crash—perhaps a fatal one.

But that mustn't happen. Because she'd promised. She'd given Francesco her solemn word, and she *must* keep it.

For herself she wasn't afraid, but she was swept with a terrible fear for him. She'd promised him, and she was about to betray him.

And then something happened that she could never afterwards explain.

She *saw* him—not as others would understand seeing, but in a way that had never happened to her before. He was there behind her eyes, a presence so intense that he was visible as nothing else had ever been. She didn't know what his face was like, but she did know the expression it wore at this moment—terrified, tortured with the effort of concealing his fear for her sake, facing a desolate future without her.

The desolation was there inside her head, too, all around her: a life that was empty because the only person who counted had gone. She had done this to him, and the knowledge of what she'd done was there, howling, shrieking at her, making her understand things to which she'd wilfully blinded herself before.

Come back to me.

Silvio's voice through the radio made her calmer.

'Lower left a bit more. You're nearly there— A bit lower—lower—'

And then there was the blessed feel of the ground as she landed heavily, going down on to her knees at once and rolling over. When she stopped she could hear the sound of distant cheering. The whole family had been watching her, their hearts in their mouths. But there was only one who mattered.

Francesco. She must get to him.

Silvio, too, had landed. Now he pulled her to her feet, got her free of the parachute and drew off her mask, freeing her face.

'They're heading this way across the airfield,' he said. 'But it's some distance.'

'Can you see Francesco?'

'He's way out in front. Here.' He took her shoulders and turned her slightly. 'He's right ahead, and there are no obstacles between you.'

'*Thanks.*'

She began walking, carefully at first, then faster, faster, running at top speed, running with total abandon, as she'd never dared to run before.

And now it was there—the rush of intoxicating joy, the glorious freedom that she'd awaited in vain during the dive.

It had come at last, possessing her as she hurtled confidently towards the arms that waited to enfold her.

'You really mean it?' he said, later that night.

They were curled up in their own bed, warm with satiated desire, and warmer still with the comfort of opening their minds and hearts to each other in a way that was new.

'I mean every word,' she assured him. 'I'm finished with all that. No more diving, jumping and suchlike.'

'You don't have to give it up now if you're not sure. I'll wait until you're ready.'

'I *am* ready. I knew that today.'

'I guess that would be about the time you were blown off course?' he said, trying to make a joke of it.

'No, it was when I landed and ran to you. I couldn't see you, but I knew you were running to me, and we'd find each other. And then I knew I didn't need anything more.'

After that there was a long silence as they held each other, not even kissing but absorbing warmth and comfort from each other's presence

'Always?' he murmured.

'Always.'

After a while he ventured to ask,

'Does that mean—no more craziness?'

'I didn't actually say that,' she said hastily. 'But there's more than one way of being crazy.'

'Well, I guess if you were sensible all the time I wouldn't know you.'

'Mum and Dad used to take risks,' she remembered. 'But they stopped when I was born. After that Dad took up sending messages into other galaxies.'

'Does he get anything back?' he asked, startled.

'Only stuff he can't understand. He'll tell you all about it when he comes for the wedding.'

He kissed her. 'What did your mother take up?'

'Me. She said I was mad enough for both of us. I'll probably find the same.'

'Are you telling me—'

'Be patient.'

Just as she thought he'd gone to sleep he murmured, 'I'm glad it happened this way.'

'Glad we quarrelled?' she asked.

'Glad we quarrelled, parted and found each other again.'

'Could it actually have been a *good* thing that I told you to get out?' she wondered, and held her breath, for the answer was important.

'Yes, or I might never have learned to confront it. You dispelled that darkness as nobody else could. And since then we've learned things about each other, and ourselves, that we needed to know.'

And solving problems was what would keep them together, she thought, glad of his wisdom.

But there was one more step before his darkness was finally banished, she thought. One more thing that only she could do.

'So now the door's open for us,' she said. 'The one that leads to the rest of our lives. Come in, my darling. *Come in.*'

Della had said that Hope's life was colourful enough to throw the other women into the shade, and it was true. She'd loved and been loved by several men, and had mothered six sons—four of them her own, two by other women. All of them looked to her as their mother.

It had been her dream to surround herself with daughters-in-law, and although the wedding of Francesco and Celia was still in the future she considered the dream fulfilled. On this day that she would share with her husband—the man who had always been her true love, even while she herself had only half known it—they would be surrounded by the children and the grandchildren they considered theirs.

Every member of the family who could manage it had travelled to Naples. Some stayed at the villa; some took rooms in nearby hotels. The celebrations had already lasted several days, as Hope had given a series of small parties so that she and Toni could spend time with everyone.

'The big party, with everyone, will be a crush,' she had told her husband. 'So packed that there will be no time for words except for speeches, which aren't the same.'

She had been right, but now the time had come she found that no words were needed. As she stood looking around the garden, where dinner was being served under coloured lamps, she saw that all her sons were there, and all the women who loved them. Beside them were their children—some fast-growing, some babies, but all providing the promise of plentiful activity, the wellspring of her life.

By now everyone knew what had happened at the hospital, and they looked at the couple walking among them with new eyes. Both were in their late sixties, together for thirty-five years, yet now they had the glow of young lovers.

There they stood, arms entwined, while the speeches proceeded and the toasts were drunk.

'And I'll swear, they never heard a word of it,' Carlo said later. 'They were in their own world and nobody else existed.'

'Did you see Franco there at all?' Della asked.

'No, he was the only person who didn't accept.'

Later that night, in the privacy of their room, Toni read again the letter his brother had written.

I know you will understand why I cannot be there. I
rejoice with you, but I'm still learning to cope with my
own loss. I'm going away for a while, to Switzerland,
where Lisa and I went on our honeymoon. I shall revisit
the places of our first happiness, and I like to think she
will be there with me, as she will always be in my heart.

Toni looked up, smiling, as his wife came and rested an arm
about his shoulder.

'Do you remember how we planned our honeymoon?' she
asked, glancing at the letter which, like Toni, she had read
many times before.

'Yes, and we never took that trip,' he remembered. 'Luke
got the flu, and then Francesco caught it from him—'

'And then I caught it, and you nursed me so tenderly,' she
recalled with a smile.

She put her other arm about him and kissed him.

'I think it's time we took that trip, *carissimo*,' she said.
'We've waited far too long.'

* * * * *

Turn the page for a sneak preview
of the first book in the new miniseries
DIAMONDS DOWN UNDER
from Silhouette Desire®,
VOWS & A VENGEFUL GROOM
by Bronwyn Jameson

Available January 2008
(SD #1843)

Silhouette Desire®
Always Powerful, Passionate and Provocative

Kimberley Blackstone didn't notice the waiting horde of media until it was too late. Flashbulbs exploded around her like a New Year's light show. She skidded to a halt, so abruptly her trailing suitcase all but overtook her.

This had to be a case of mistaken identity. Surely. Kimberley hadn't been on the paparazzi hit list for close to a decade, not since she'd estranged herself from her billionaire father and his headline-hungry diamond business.

But no, it was *her* name they called. *Her* face was the focus of a swarm of lenses that circled her like avid hornets. Her heart started to pound with fear-fueled adrenaline.

What did they want?

What was going on?

With a rising sense of bewilderment she scanned the crowd for a clue, and her gaze fastened on a tall, leonine figure forcing his way to the front. A tall, familiar figure. Her head came up in stunned recognition, and their gazes collided across the sea of heads before the cameras erupted with another barrage of flashes, this time right in her exposed face.

Blinded by the flashbulbs—and by the shock of that momentary eye-meet—Kimberley didn't realize his intent until he'd forged his way to her side, possibly by the sheer strength of his personality. She felt his arm wrap around her shoulder, pulling her into the protective shelter of his body, allowing her no time to object. No chance to lift her hands to ward him off.

In the space of a hastily drawn breath, she found herself plastered knee-to-nose against six feet two inches of hard-bodied male.

Ric Perrini.

Her lover for ten torrid weeks, her husband for ten tumultuous days.

Her ex for ten tranquil years.

After all this time, he should not have felt so familiar but, oh dear, he did. She knew the scent of that body and its lean, muscular strength. She knew its heat and its slick power and every response it could draw from hers.

She also recognized the ease with which he'd taken control of the moment and the decisiveness of his deep voice when it rumbled close to her ear. "I have a car waiting outside. Is this your only luggage?"

Kimberley nodded. "I assume you will tell me," she said tightly, "what this welcome party is all about."

"Not while the welcome party is within earshot. No."

Barking a request for the cameramen to stand aside, Perrini took her hand and pulled her into step with his ground-eating stride. Kimberley let him, because he was right, damn his arrogant, Italian-suited hide. Despite the speed with which he whisked her across the airport terminal, she could almost feel the hot breath of the pursuing media on her back.

This was neither the time nor the place for explanations. Inside his car, however, she would get answers.

Now that the initial shock had been blown away—by the haste of their retreat, by the heat of her gathering indignation, by the rush of adrenaline fired by Perrini's presence and the looming verbal battle—her brain was starting to tick over. This had to be her father's doing. And if it was a Howard Blackstone publicity ploy, then it had to be about Blackstone Diamonds, the company that ruled his life.

The knowledge made her chest tighten with a familiar ache of disillusionment.

She'd known her father would be flying in from Sydney for today's opening of the newest in his chain of exclusive, high-end jewelry boutiques. The opulent shopfront sat adjacent to the rival business where Kimberley worked. No coincidence, she thought bitterly, just as it was no coincidence that Ric Perrini was here in Auckland ushering her to his car.

Perrini was Howard Blackstone's right-hand man, second in command at Blackstone Diamonds, a legacy of his short-lived marriage to the boss's daughter. No doubt her father had sent him to fetch her; the question was *why?*

* * * * *

Get swept away down under with the glitz and glamour of the Blackstone empire as Kimberley tries to determine the real reason behind her "reunion" with Ric....

Look for *VOWS & A VENGEFUL GROOM*
by Bronwyn Jameson,
in stores January 2008.

When Kimberley Blackstone's father is
presumed dead, Kimberley is required to take
over the helm of Blackstone Diamonds. She
has to work closely with her ex, Ric Perrini, to
battle not only the press, but also the fierce
attraction still sizzling between them. Does Ric
feel the same...or is it the power her share of
Blackstone Diamonds will provide him as he
battles for boardroom supremacy.

Look for

VOWS &
A VENGEFUL GROOM
by

BRONWYN
JAMESON

Available January wherever you buy books

To fulfill his father's dying wish,
Greek tycoon Christos Niarchos must
marry Ava Monroe, a woman who
betrayed him years ago. But his soon-to-
be-wife has a secret that could rock
more than his passion for her.

Look for

THE GREEK TYCOON'S SECRET HEIR

by

KATHERINE GARBERA

Available January wherever you buy books

REQUEST YOUR FREE BOOKS!
2 FREE NOVELS PLUS 2
FREE GIFTS!

HARLEQUIN ROMANCE®

From the Heart, For the Heart

YES! Please send me 2 FREE Harlequin Romance® novels and my 2 FREE gifts. After receiving them, if I don't wish to receive any more books, I can return the shipping statement marked "cancel." If I don't cancel, I will receive 4 brand-new novels every month and be billed just $3.57 per book in the U.S., or $4.05 per book in Canada, plus 25¢ shipping and handling per book and applicable taxes, if any*. That's a savings of over 15% off the cover price! I understand that accepting the 2 free books and gifts places me under no obligation to buy anything. I can always return a shipment and cancel at any time. Even if I never buy another book from Harlequin, the two free books and gifts are mine to keep forever.

114 HDN EEV7 314 HDN EEWK

Name	(PLEASE PRINT)
Address	Apt.
City	State/Prov.	Zip/Postal Code

Signature (if under 18, a parent or guardian must sign)

Mail to the Harlequin Reader Service®:
IN U.S.A.: P.O. Box 1867, Buffalo, NY 14240-1867
IN CANADA: P.O. Box 609, Fort Erie, Ontario L2A 5X3

Not valid to current Harlequin Romance subscribers.

Want to try two free books from another line?
Call 1-800-873-8635 or visit www.morefreebooks.com.

* Terms and prices subject to change without notice. NY residents add applicable sales tax. Canadian residents will be charged applicable provincial taxes and GST. This offer is limited to one order per household. All orders subject to approval. Credit or debit balances in a customer's account(s) may be offset by any other outstanding balance owed by or to the customer. Please allow 4 to 6 weeks for delivery.

Your Privacy: Harlequin is committed to protecting your privacy. Our Privacy Policy is available online at www.eHarlequin.com or upon request from the Reader Service. From time to time we make our lists of customers available to reputable firms who may have a product or service of interest to you. If you would prefer we not share your name and address, please check here. ☐

HR07

Inside ROMANCE

Stay up-to-date on all your romance reading news!

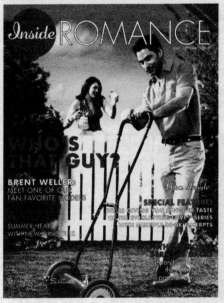

Inside Romance is a FREE quarterly newsletter highlighting our upcoming series releases and promotions.

Visit
www.eHarlequin.com/InsideRomance
to sign up to receive our complimentary newsletter today!

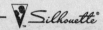

HARLEQUIN *Romance*

Coming Next Month

**Start your New Year with a bang with six terrific reads,
only from Harlequin Romance®.**

#3997 HER HAND IN MARRIAGE Jessica Steele
Get ready for the perfect English gentleman to sweep you off your feet!
Romillie never imagined that a high-flying executive like Naylor would
be interested in an ordinary girl like her, but she's bowled over when he
whisks her away to his beautiful Cotswold cottage....

#3998 THE RANCHER'S DOORSTEP BABY Patricia Thayer
Western Weddings
Does the image of a man cradling a tiny baby in his arms melt your heart?
You aren't alone! Rachel isn't sure whether drifter Cole will stick around for
long, but seeing the tender way he holds her delicate baby, she knows her
heart belongs to him forever.

#3999 THE SHEIKH'S UNSUITABLE BRIDE Liz Fielding
Desert Brides
Have you ever wanted someone you really shouldn't have? Desert prince
Zahir knows Diana is not what his family and country expect in a wife. But
this thoroughly unsuitable woman, whose eyes sparkle with mischief, is
worth breaking the rules for.

#4000 THE BRIDESMAID'S BEST MAN Barbara Hannay
One special night between rugged best man Mark and beautiful
bridesmaid Sophie seemed to be all they would get to share, as Mark had
to return home to Australia. But now it seems these two will be sharing the
most special job of all—parenthood!

#4001 MOONLIGHT AND ROSES Jackie Braun
Jaye thought she knew what she wanted from life—her career, and the
freedom to be her own woman. But the intoxicating mix of new business
partner Zack, the glimmer of moonlight and the scent of roses in the air is
making her change her mind....

#4002 A MOTHER IN A MILLION Melissa James
Heart to Heart
How can you be sure that someone loves you—really loves *you*?
Jennifer's heart goes out to single dad Noah and his motherless children,
but when he proposes, Jennifer wants to be sure he wants her as his wife,
not just as a mother to his children.